Hi

D1462966

Nadina remembe~~~ ~~~~~~~~~ ~~~~ ~~~~ ~~~~
her and shivered.

Lyle's arms tightened around her.

"It is all right," he said.

He nearly added: " . . . because I love you!"

Then he told himself that she was relying on
him as a child relies on its father.

What he must do was to make her feel safe
and not trouble her with any other emotion.

At the same time, it was a bitter-sweet feeling
to hold her gently when he wanted to crush her
in his arms.

To kiss her with passionate, demanding kisses
until she kissed him in return!

A Camfield Novel of Love
by Barbara Cartland

———

*"Barbara Cartland's novels are all distinguished by their
intelligence, good sense, and good nature...."*

—ROMANTIC TIMES

*"Who could give better advice on how to keep your romance
going strong than the world's most famous romance novelist, Barbara Cartland?"*

—THE STAR

Camfield Place,
Hatfield
Hertfordshire,
England

Dearest Reader,

Camfield Novels of Love mark a very exciting era of my books with Jove. They have already published nearly two hundred of my titles since they became my first publisher in America, and now all my original paperback romances in the future will be published exclusively by them.

As you already know, Camfield Place in Hertfordshire is my home, which originally existed in 1275, but was rebuilt in 1867 by the grandfather of Beatrix Potter.

It was here in this lovely house, with the best view in the county, that she wrote *The Tale of Peter Rabbit*. Mr. McGregor's garden is exactly as she described it. The door in the wall that the fat little rabbit could not squeeze underneath and the goldfish pool where the white cat sat twitching its tail are still there.

I had Camfield Place blessed when I came here in 1950 and was so happy with my husband until he died, and now with my children and grandchildren, that I know the atmosphere is filled with love and we have all been very lucky.

It is easy here to write of love and I know you will enjoy the Camfield Novels of Love. Their plots are definitely exciting and the covers very romantic. They come to you, like all my books, with love.

Bless you,

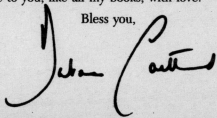

CAMFIELD NOVELS OF LOVE

by Barbara Cartland

A NEW CAMFIELD NOVEL OF LOVE BY

BARBARA CARTLAND

Hidden by Love

JOVE BOOKS, NEW YORK

HIDDEN BY LOVE

A Jove Book / published by arrangement with the author

PRINTING HISTORY
Jove edition / November 1992

ISBN: 0-515-10983-5

Jove Books are published by The Berkley Publishing Group,
200 Madison Avenue, New York, New York 10016.
The name "JOVE" and the "J" logo
are trademarks belonging to Jove Publications, Inc.

PRINTED IN THE UNITED STATES OF AMERICA

10 9 8 7 6 5 4 3 2 1

Author's Note

WHEN I visited Turkey first in 1927 the country was very poor, and a great number of people in the streets of Constantinople were Russians who had fled from the Revolution in 1917.

My husband and I were on a cruise in the Mediterranean and were warned by the Captain of the ship to be careful of what we ate and drank.

I was, however, thrilled by the beauty of the City and I saw the Harem for the first time, and enjoyed the Bazaar.

The second time I went to Turkey was with my two sons in 1976 and everything in the country was better, although there was evidence of poverty.

But we were thrilled when we crossed the Dardanelles in a Ferry, as I do in this novel, and went down the coast, visiting Troy and other places of ancient interest.

Ephesis was sheer delight and I have never forgotten the beauty and history of it.

I have now been to Turkey for the third time, and everything was different.

The huge Hotels that have gone up are as comfortable and luxurious as any in Europe, the Bosporus just as beautiful, and the people looked well and happy and are very welcoming.

I was delighted to learn that thirty per cent of the Turkish women read my novels.

Although a number of them have been plagiarised, they are done very well, so it was delightful to see them.

I drove along the side of the Bosporus, and it was in fact the Summer Palace of the Sultans which gave me the introduction for this novel.

The whole story came to me as I drove to where I could see the opening of the Bosporus into the Black Sea.

My younger son and I had a very happy five days in Turkey, and the kindness and friendliness of everybody we met made us determined to return as soon as possible.

Hidden by Love

chapter one

1875

THE child in Nadina's arms fell asleep.

She was only four and she had been playing and learning all the morning.

Nadina rocked her very gently.

The dazzling sunshine was reflected in a million points of light on the blue seas of the Bosporus.

It was one of the only places in the world where the sea came right up to the land.

There was no pebbled beach.

In front of the terrace on which Nadina was sitting the water was lapping against the sides of the garden.

Earlier she had shown the child in her arms the fish swimming below them.

Her thoughts went back to her own childhood and she started to sing a Lullaby.

Her Nanny had sung it to her when she was the same age as little Rahmi.

Because she was a Muslim the child had a great number of names.

Her dark hair curled round her small chubby face.

Her eyes, which were very large and were now closed, were full of intelligence.

Nadina loved teaching Rahmi.

She thought to herself as she sang that she was fortunate to have found somewhere safe, somewhere where she would not be found.

Then the soft notes of her voice went out as if on the wind.

The English words seemed somehow appropriate to the Fairylike view ahead.

Suddenly Nadina stiffened.

A man's head had appeared directly in front of her, just above the terrace.

"Help me," he pleaded in English. "For God's sake, help me! They are right behind me!"

For a second Nadina just stared at him.

Then, as if some Power beyond herself told her what to do, she said:

"There are clothes in there."

As she spoke she pointed to the small building that was little larger than a Temple.

Her employer, Nannk Osman, used it when he swam in the Bosporus.

He was a youngish man, and he enjoyed the water even when it was cold.

Instead of running back to the big house that he had built as a summer residence, he found it more convenient to have a place by the water.

There he could dry himself and dress.

Without replying, the man who had spoken to

Nadina in English heaved himself up deftly onto the terrace.

Moving incredibly swiftly, he disappeared into the small building which Nadina had indicated.

He left behind him a large splash of water on the white stones.

With the instinct of somebody who has had to hide and learnt to leave no suspicious marks behind her, Nadina rose.

Carrying the child with one hand, she threw a white shawl over the wet stones.

She had pulled it over Rahmi's legs when she fell asleep.

Then she went back and sat down, aware that her heart was beating.

She was apprehensive and afraid.

It was not long before she knew the reason for her fear.

A large *Caique* came in sight with six men rowing it.

Nadina realised at once that it had come from the Black Sea.

The opening from the Bosporus was not far from the garden.

Undoubtedly the men in it were Russians.

They were taking a chance coming into the Bosporus.

Since the Crimean War, Russia was the avowed enemy of Turkey.

This was something that was encouraged by most of the Powers of Europe.

None of them wished to see Russia expand or grow stronger.

England was fiercely guarding her route to India.

The *Caique* came alongside the terrace and Nadina stared at the men.

The six rowing the *Caique* were the large, hearty Serfs that one expected to find in the South of Russia.

There were, however, two men seated in the stern who, she knew at a glance, were very different.

She thought their peaked faces and suspicious eyes were typical of the Third Section.

They responsible for some of the atrocities that had been committed in the Balkans in the name of freedom.

Always ready to stir up trouble, the Russians seemed to be everywhere.

It was with a feeling of relief that the Turks, who had not suffered much from the Crimean War, could now throw them out of Constantinople.

They wanted, instead, to be friendly with Europe.

Three of the men who had been rowing the *Caique* held on to the side of the terrace.

The two who had been seated in the stern stepped into the garden.

They looked at Nadina, and one man said in Turkish:

"A man came here! Where is he?"

Nadina hesitated for a moment, wondering if she should answer him in the same language.

French was the language used by all the intelligentsia in Russia.

At the Court of St. Petersburg no one of quality spoke any other language.

After a moment she said slowly in French:

"*Non*, there is no man, and you have no right to come here. This is the private house of Consular Nannk Osman."

The two men looked at each other.

Then one replied to Nadina in the language in which she spoke to him.

"That is not the truth, *Mademoiselle*. We are sure this is where the man stopped."

"I do not know who you are talking about," Nadina said, "but if you trespass on this land I will send for the guards. They are not far away in the house and will come at once if I call them."

She saw the men's eyes flicker.

She knew they had no wish to be involved with the Turkish guards.

They would undoubtedly consider it an outrage that they should enter the garden without permission.

"Go away!" Nadina said, "and go quietly or you will wake this child who is the pride and joy of the Consular's eyes."

The men did not move.

One, however, looked round, peering through the bushes.

Then the other looked at the small building into which the Englishman had vanished.

Nadina felt she must play for time.

"Tell me," she said, "was the man you are seeking swimming?"

"*Oui, oui!*" one of the Russians answered. "He was swimming. Did you see him?"

"I thought I saw a man pass by here a short while ago," Nadina replied. "He was swimming very strongly."

5

"Where did he go?"

Nadina rose slowly from her chair.

Carrying the still-sleeping child to the edge of the landing place, she pointed.

It was in the direction of Constantinople.

The two Russians whispered to each other.

Moving slowly, she went back to the chair and sat down again.

It was then one of the men made a sudden movement towards the small building to the left of them.

Nadina gave a cry.

"No, you must not go in there!" she said. "It is forbidden!"

The Russian looked back at her.

Then, as if he thought she was only a tiresome woman defying him, he passed through the opening.

Nadina held her breath.

She could only pray that the Englishman had hidden himself.

The Russian, however, was confronted by something he had not expected.

Lying on a divan, which was heaped with cushions, was a very large Turk.

He was wearing a dressing-gown over ballooning pantaloons.

On his head was a red fez and his pipe was beside him.

But for the moment he was asleep.

His face was turned against the cushions, one arm thrown over his chin as if to hide his head.

It was hard to see him clearly, as the sunblinds were drawn over the windows.

He was snoring and the sound seemed to echo round the small room.

The Russian stood staring at him.

Then he realised he had made a mistake.

He moved silently back the way he had come.

The other Russian had not moved, but was standing beside Nadina.

The man coming from the small building shook his head.

Without a word they both hurried towards the *Caique* and stepped into it.

They gave an order and the oarsmen pulled out into the sea.

They did not go in the way Nadina had pointed.

They merely swung round and started back towards the Black Sea.

Nadina felt a feeling of relief sweep over her.

She was weak with the intensity of it.

She knew exactly what would have happened if the Russians had found the man they were seeking.

He would have been dragged aboard the *Caique*.

They would have taken him with them, doubtless for interrogation and the inevitable torture that went with it.

She had saved him by a hair's-breadth.

As the Russian had not spoken, she had no idea what he had found in the small building, whether the Englishman had hidden or had somehow managed to deceive him.

The Englishman did not appear.

After waiting and listening until it became intolerable, Nadina rose to her feet.

Walking towards the entrance of the small building, still holding the child in her arms, she asked:

"Are you there? They have gone!"

There was a moment before the answer came:

"Are you quite certain of that?"

"They have returned to the Black Sea."

"Then I must thank God, and you, for saving me," the Englishman answered.

Nadina paused.

Then she asked:

"Have you got everything you want?"

As she spoke she wondered that, if the answer was 'No,' what she could do about it?

It would be a great mistake for the servants in the house to know there was a stranger in the garden.

Fortunately, at this time of day they were, like all their countrymen, taking a *siesta* after the midday meal.

Even the guards would be sleeping instead of patrolling the garden as they were supposed to do.

There was really no danger they needed to anticipate.

However, every Turk of great importance had guards around his Palace or his house.

Nannk Osman was very important indeed.

He was the largest supplier of provisions which were now for the first time pouring into Turkey from the rest of Europe.

In return, Europe purchased grapes, pears, pomegranates, vegetables, and fish which brought in much-needed money to Constantinople.

Osman had started life frying, on a portable stove in the crowded street, oysters caught that morning with iron rakes.

He also sold pilaffs stuffed with cucumbers, hagis, and the very popular tripe.

Soon he had one shop in the Bazaar, then several outside in the City and more and more each year.

Change had come swiftly to Constantinople, so swiftly that even now a great number of the Elders could hardly believe it possible.

Yet the last Sultan had altered everything at an unbelievable speed.

Abdulmecit had minted coins.

He built the first bridge across the Golden Horn.

Then, to the dismay of many old-fashioned Turks, he had reformed the National Dress.

Overnight, it seemed, their romantic ballooning pantaloons, the sable-trimmed Kaftans, and the two-foot-high turbans vanished.

They were replaced by all the Officials wearing tight black trousers, the *Stambouline* with a dull black frock-coat and, of course, the fez.

It was the method of dress that had originated in Morocco.

What one man wore, another man must.

Regardless of protest, Western dress had come to stay.

What worried Nadina now was whether her employer had left these clothes in what was actually his bathing-cabin.

Because it was easier, he often, when he was at home, wore the old Turkish loose garments.

She had seen him wearing them in the morning when he hurried down to swim.

She was, however, afraid that the Englishman would have found nothing in which to clothe his nakedness.

Then, as she waited for him to speak, he came from behind her.

She gave a little gasp at his appearance.

He was a tall man, but fortunately Nannk Osman was also big and broad-shouldered.

He was wearing the black trousers and the *Stambouline*.

His shirt was somewhat peculiar.

It was one of the loose white garments Nannk Osman wore for comfort.

But Nadina could see now that he was a very handsome man.

His dark hair was brushed back from a square forehead.

He had clear-cut features which were very English.

"How can I thank you," he asked in a low voice, "for saving my life?"

"It was fortunate that I was here," she answered, "but they have gone now and will, I think, be too nervous to return."

"I can only thank you from the bottom of my heart," the Englishman said. "It was very clever of you to delay them as you did. I realised as I listened that that was what you were doing."

"I was so afraid," Nadina said, "that you would not find any clothes like you have on now in which you can leave here."

"I will return them the moment I can find my own things," the Englishman replied.

Nadina thought for a moment.

"The owner of this house," she said, "is away for another three days. If you can put them back without anybody being aware of it, it would save a great deal of explanation."

The Englishman looked at her penetratingly.

It was as if he thought she had some particular reason for asking this.

Then he smiled.

"Of course I will do anything you ask me to do," he said. "I can say only that I am astonished that any young woman could be so quick-witted, and help me without needing explanations, which, of course, might have proved fatal."

"I have had some experience of having to hide," Nadina answered with a smile.

"Why should you hide?" the Englishman asked. "I thought that after the war the English were most welcome in Turkey."

Nadina looked away from him.

Then she said:

"I am not English, I am French. My name is Nadina Revon."

"Then, *Mademoiselle* Revon, I salute you!" the Englishman exclaimed.

They were outside in the garden before he said:

"I think, in case anyone in the house awakes from their *siesta*, I should be on my way."

"If you are going to Constantinople, how will you manage?" Nadina asked.

"You must not worry about me," he replied. "I am used to looking after myself, but I promise you that the clothes will be returned and no one else will have the slightest idea that I have borrowed them."

"Thank you."

She thought the Englishman was about to move away; then he hesitated before he said:

"It seems wrong that I have nothing to give you to express my gratitude. My name is Lyle Westley,

11

and if you are ever in trouble or need my services, they will know at the British Embassy how to find me. If I am not there, they will assist you in any way they can."

"Thank you," Nadina smiled.

She put out her hand, still holding the child with her arm.

He took it in his.

Then, to her surprise, he bent his head.

He actually touched the softness of her skin before be said:

"Thank you again, *Mademoiselle*, and God bless you."

He released her hand, then turned and walked away among the bushes.

He seemed, she thought, to know by instinct the part of the garden in which he would not be seen.

If he walked to the very end of it, he could quite easily swing himself over the fence into the road.

He would, however, have no money.

She wondered if she ought to have lent him some.

Then she was quite certain that the one thing he wanted more than anything else was to feel free, not only of the Russians, but from everybody.

Any unnecessary contact could be dangerous.

Any more things to be returned than were absolutely necessary might lead to questions and investigations.

She was still standing looking after him when little Rahmi moved from her arms.

Rubbing her eyes, she said in Turkish:

"Tell me a story."

"Ask me in French," Nadina replied.

A little hesitatingly the child said the words.

Nadina kissed her.

"You are a very clever girl!" she said. "When your Father comes back, he will be very proud of how much you have learnt."

The little girl was very quick-witted and indeed, Nadina thought, took after her Father.

She had only to look at the large, magnificent house he had built to guess how much money he had made.

Other Turks were suffering a penury they did not deserve.

Things were in fact very bad in Constantinople.

The war had prevented the Russians from invading Turkey.

Yet the whole country had been invaded by something even more unscrupulous—the European Money-Lender.

Abdul Aziz was the first Sultan of the Ottoman Empire to fall into the clutches of the Financiers of Western Europe.

He had borrowed money, vast sums, to modernise his Armies.

He occupied the most enormous and extravagant Palace in the whole world—the Dolmabahce, and had built another at Beylerbey, across the Bosporus.

The Dolmabahce Palace was a building decorated with gold. It dazzled those who observed it.

Yet there was bound to be a day of reckoning.

In the meantime, Abdul Aziz spent money in a way that had never been dreamt of before.

The number of his Concubines increased to 900 and they were guarded by 3,000 black eunuchs.

Everything else about him was, like his physique,

large and, in fact, over-powering.

He himself was probably the finest of his race for over 400 years.

He slept in an eight-foot-long bed.

It was wide enough to accommodate, not only his enormous frame, but also one or more of his Concubines.

Everyone in Constantinople watched the Sultan's wild extravagance.

They found it hard to believe that it was actually happening.

The European Powers were eager to support any country that was within reach of the Russians' greedy claws.

Abdul Aziz was invited on a State visit to Paris.

In France the Second Empire with its glories and extravagance was drawing to a close.

But the Great Exhibition was attracting Monarchs and Consorts from every corner of Europe.

Never had such a galaxy of crowned heads been seen in one Capital at the same time.

Abdul Aziz was fêted by Louis Napoleon with a wild extravagance which he understood.

The Emperor transformed the Élysée Palace into the Fairyland of the Arabian Nights in his honour.

The Sultan went on to stay in England.

After a great deal of argument with her Ministers, Queen Victoria agreed to come out of retirement and receive him.

The streets of London were lined with cheering crowds.

Although the Crimean War was long over, they could still remember that they had a gallant ally in Turkey.

The Sultan was invited to dine at Guildhall.

Determined not to be outdone, he arrived on a white Charger, his uniform glittering with medals.

He wore an egret of diamonds on his fez.

The effect of all this European hospitality was to make Abdul Aziz more extravagant than ever.

The amount he spent on the Dolmabahce Palace on his return was over two-million pounds.

He had a staff of 5,000 servants.

He entertained on the most lavish scale in Ottoman history.

His dinner parties usually meant that he invited 300 or more guests.

He greeted them with 400 musicians.

The men looking after his menagerie numbered 200.

There were 300 cooks in the Kitchen and 400 grooms in the Stables.

The splendours of Europe had impressed Abdul Aziz so much that he engaged in a new burst of spending.

From Paris he ordered a solid gold dinner-service encrusted with rubies and emeralds.

He had the walls of his Palace panelled in mother-of-pearl.

From Britain he bought dozens of pianos.

They were played in the Palace gardens strapped to men's backs so that he could be followed with music when he took a stroll.

He also purchased locomotives from Britain.

There were, however, no tracks on which they could run.

He then gave an order for five Battleships, although he had no sailors to man them.

Nadina listened, as did everybody else, to the stories that circulated round Constantinople.

She hoped that she would never have to meet the Sultan.

She had found a little haven with Nannk Osman after her father died.

Unless she was very unlucky, she could stay with him for years.

Because he was progressive, he was determined that his children should speak several languages.

They started with French.

This was why he had engaged Nadina.

French was to be followed by English, Italian, and some of the more useful of the Balkan languages.

It was certainly an innovation that such an extensive education should be given to a girl.

His sons, whom he had by his first two wives, were taught by male Tutors.

He was wildly attached to his pretty daughter.

He was determined she should be a Queen amongst the modern women who were just beginning to emerge in Turkey.

They still wore the *yashmak*.

Yet in many cases it was little more than a piece of gauze.

It was the Sultan's idea that his Concubines should go to the shops rather than that the goods be brought to them.

Nadina often found it easier to wear a *yashmak* and a *burnouse*.

Otherwise she was stared at, and it was a mistake to go alone.

At the same time, Europeans were coming to

Constantinople in large numbers.

Amongst them were quite a number of distin-guished women.

"Soon no one will notice me," she told herself.

That was what she wanted above all else.

When she was quite certain that Lyle Westley had got away, she walked slowly back to the house.

As she expected, the door-keeper was asleep.

He awoke with a start as she reached the door.

He got to his feet reluctantly.

She passed him and went up the stairs.

Beautiful rooms had been allotted to Rahmi.

The child ran ahead of her to look for her favourite doll.

Nadina went to a window.

From there she could see almost to the end of the garden.

The view was partly obscured by a number of trees that were in blossom.

Searching the ground, she saw no one.

Lyle Westley was on his way to Constantinople.

She supposed he would find some vehicle to convey him there.

But, as he had no money when he arrived, she guessed he would go to the British Embassy.

Perhaps he would find some way of changing.

She knew that those who had to hide themselves were very careful.

They did not want to be seen in a disguise that could be recognised as something out of the ordinary.

One false step, or mistake, might mean death.

It would be foolish, therefore, to leave anything to chance.

'He was very good-looking,' she thought.

She wondered if she would ever see him again.

Then she laughed at the mere idea.

He was doubtless only passing through Turkey.

The only place he could have come from was Russia.

If he had been in Russia, which obviously he had, he must have been spying.

Nothing could be more dangerous.

The Russians were suspicious even of their own shadows.

Their Secret Service operated everywhere and nobody was safe from their investigations.

"I am so glad that I could help him get away," Nadina told herself.

She prayed that he would be safe and never again be in such a tight spot.

Now that it was all over, she began to feel a little weak.

Everything could have gone wrong.

She might have failed him.

The Russians might not have waited to talk to her before searching the place where he was hiding.

She felt it would have been unbearable to see him dragged away, perhaps knocked into unconsciousness before they threw him into the *Caique*.

She thought she could see the Russians still, like a dark overwhelming menace.

'Be careful! Be . . . careful!'

She sent her thoughts towards Lyle Westley as if on wings.

Then she told herself to be sensible.

There was nothing more she could do, and doubtless he would never think of her again.

Then, as Rahmi called to her, she looked down at her hand.

He had touched it with his lips.

It was the first kiss she had ever had from a man.

chapter two

A servant announced from the door:

"A Gentleman to see you, Sir."

The British Ambassador looked up from his desk.

"Who is it?" he asked. "I am very busy."

"Mr. Westley, Sir."

"Westley?" the Ambassador exclaimed. "Send him in immediately!"

Lyle Westley walked into the Ambassador's Private Room.

He was wearing his red fez and the clothes in which he had left Nadina.

Walter Baring stared at him in astonishment.

Then he burst out laughing.

"I do not believe it!" he exclaimed. "Where the hell have you been?"

"I want to send a cable to London immediately!" Lyle Westley replied. "Then I will tell you everything."

"They have been screaming for you for the last

month," the Ambassador said, "so I only hope you have something to tell them."

"I have everything the Prime Minister is waiting to hear," Lyle Westley said quietly.

He pulled off his fez, which he had worn only to surprise the Ambassador, and threw it down on a chair.

Then, as Walter Baring pressed a special button on his desk, the door opened.

One of his Senior Assistants came in.

"Westley is back, thank God!" the Ambassador said. "Have him taken immediately to the Cable Room."

"Of course, Sir," the Assistant replied.

He smiled at Lyle Westley, saying:

"It is a good thing you have turned up. Everybody's been screeching like peacocks and I began to think your luck in staying alive had run out!"

"I was saved by a hair's-breadth," Lyle Westley answered, "by a rather beautiful creature with fair hair and blue eyes."

As he was speaking he walked from the room and the Assistant followed him.

"That would happen to you," he said ruefully. "If it had been me, I would have been saved by some old scarecrow with white hair and no teeth!"

The two men were laughing as they went into a locked room.

It was where special cables in code were sent to the Foreign Office.

The Ambassador waited impatiently.

It was over half-an-hour before Lyle Westley returned.

As he sat down in an armchair by the fireplace, the Ambassador said:

"We are celebrating your return with a glass of champagne."

He walked to a side-table.

A bottle was standing in a silver ice-bucket. He poured out a glass and handed it to Lyle Westley.

Then he filled one for himself.

"Seriously, Westley," he said, "I was beginning to feel frightened about what had happened to you."

"I was somewhat frightened myself," Lyle Westley replied.

He drank some of the champagne before he went on:

"I wanted that! But what I need more than anything else is sleep!"

"There is a bed-room waiting for you upstairs," Walter Baring replied.

"Thank you." Lyle Westley smiled. "As you see, I also want to change into my own clothes, which I imagine you still have hidden away somewhere."

"They are as safe here as anything is safe in Turkey at the moment," Walter Baring answered, "with the Sultan growing more insane every day."

Lyle Westley raised his eye-brows.

"As bad as that?"

"Worse! We are never quite certain what he will do next. His staff are all terrified of him, as you can imagine."

Lyle took another sip of the champagne.

"You must tell me all about it," he said, "when I can concentrate on something other than keeping my head on my shoulders."

"I will let you go to bed the minute you tell me

what you have discovered."

"Exactly what you expected," Lyle answered. "The Bulgarians have suffered enough and are on the verge of collapse."

Walter Baring pressed his lips together.

It was to prevent himself from saying it was what he had suspected.

"The Russians, who as we know are always eager to stir up trouble," Lyle went on, "are doing their damnedest to make the revolt as large and as overwhelming as possible."

"You have advised London of this?" the Ambassador asked.

"That, and a great deal more," Lyle replied, "and now, if Your Excellency will forgive me, I can just manage to stagger upstairs before I fall asleep."

"I will see that you manage it and have everything you require," Walter Baring said.

He rang the bell.

A servant opened the door immediately and the Ambassador said:

"Take Mr. Westley up to his room and look after him. See that he is not disturbed until he wakes."

The servant bowed and Lyle Westley followed him from the room.

When he was alone the Ambassador sighed.

It was what they had expected and what he feared.

He knew that anything Lyle Westley had discovered would be correct, but he was wondering what he personally could do about it.

Ordinarily, he would have contacted the Sultan.

They would have planned together how to prevent Russia from making the most, as she always did, of any difficulties in the Balkans.

At this particular moment, however, as he well knew, the whole Ottoman Empire was ripe for revolt.

The misery of the majority of people had been made worse by the two bad harvests.

He had known for some months there was bound to be an explosion.

The Russians would take every advantage of it.

Britain must guard the Suez Canal—it was the gateway to India.

He got up from his desk and walked about the room.

He was wishing with every fibre of his being that he could discuss this further with Lyle Westley.

Yet, he knew, by the tired expression in his eyes and the way he had spoken, that he had been through a traumatic experience.

He must give him time to recover.

Lyle Westley had become a legend.

He was a young man who could have spent his time enjoying the Social Life in London.

Instead, he had chosen to be one of the courageous men who served the Empire.

He had become one of the most brilliant of those who, to put it bluntly, spied on Britain's enemies.

It was an incredibly brave decision to take.

They risked torture or death almost every day of their lives.

Lyle Westley came from an ancient and very respected family.

His father, the 6th Baronet, owned a large estate in Huntingdonshire and was a very rich man.

He had naturally expected that his eldest son

would follow him in having some very fine race-horses and training them at Newmarket.

He thought, too, that Lyle would take over the estate.

It had been in the family for nearly four-hundred years.

Instead, Lyle served first as a soldier in India.

Inevitably he became one of the players in the "Great Game."

This was the most ingenious and brilliant Secret Service network ever known.

When he decided to leave the Army, it was because he wanted to offer his services to the Foreign Office.

They jumped at the opportunity.

They desperately needed help in their extremely difficult task in expanding the Empire, at the same time, to try, insofar as it was possible, to avoid war.

The Crimean War had been a disaster.

This was not only because of the loss of so many men.

The horror of the way the wounded and sick had suffered was exposed by Florence Nightingale.

On top of this, Russia, who had the most incompetent, undisciplined Army in the world, had been the victor.

It had given the Russians ambitions for expansion.

This was dangerous, particularly to the Sultan.

The Russians had always been a nuisance in India by stirring up trouble between Afghanistan and the North-West Frontier.

Now there was no doubt Russia had her eye on the Ottoman Empire.

The Ambassador realised he was in the "hot seat."

He could only hope that Lyle would not sleep for too long.

As it happened, Lyle Westley did not move for twenty-four hours.

When he did, he had something to eat, then went back to sleep again.

He finally awoke the following afternoon feeling rested and able to think clearly.

Tired though he had been, he had remembered, when taking off his borrowed clothes, that they must be returned before their owner realized they were missing.

This had been arranged through the Ambassador's private servant.

Almost Lyle's first question on waking, when he rang the bell for a bath, was:

"Did the clothes I was wearing go back as I instructed?"

"Yes, Master," the man replied. "They were taken late at night and placed in the building you described."

"The man was not seen or questioned?" Lyle Westley enquired sharply.

The servant shook his head.

"He very experienced man—walk like shadow—no one see or hear."

That was all Lyle Westley wanted to know.

He thought with satisfaction that the operation had been completed without there being any repercussions.

As he dressed, he remembered the girl who had helped him.

27

She had been very intelligent about it.

Also, she was one of the loveliest young women he had seen for a long time.

At that moment, however, he had not thought of her in any way except as a miracle.

She had saved him from destruction with only seconds to spare.

'Perhaps I should send her flowers, or a present!' he thought as he fastened his waistcoat.

Then he told himself that would be extremely dangerous not only to her, but also to himself.

The Russians may have lost him for the moment.

He was, however, quite certain they would have alerted their spies in Constantinople.

He would be lucky if he was not spirited away when he was unattended.

If he walked along the crowded streets, there was always the chance of a dagger being thrust into his back.

He went down the stairs.

As he did so, he knew that he would be foolish to remain in Constantinople.

* * *

Nadina dared not look inside the bathing-hut in the garden for two days.

When she thought Nannk Osman might be returning, she went into it with Rahmi.

The first thing she saw was the red fez.

Then, hanging beside a dressing-gown was the *Stambouline*.

She was so delighted that the sunshine seemed brighter and the birds were singing.

Lyle Westley had not failed her and there would be no trouble about the missing clothes.

It also meant that he had reached his destination safely.

That, she supposed, was the British Embassy.

Just as Lyle Westley was aware that the Russians were everywhere, so was Nadina.

"He must be careful . . . very careful!" she said to herself.

As she had done before, she said a little prayer for his safety.

That afternoon she was bringing Rahmi down from the bed-room, where she had slept after luncheon.

As she did so, there was a sound below them.

The child looked over the bannisters.

"Papa! Papa!" she cried out.

Before Nadina could stop her, she had run down the stairs to fling herself into her Father's arms.

He picked her up, kissed her, then, holding her tightly in his arms, asked:

"Have you been a good girl while I have been away, and have you missed me?"

"You are back! You are back!" Rahmi replied. "Did you bring Rahmi a present?"

"I have a dozen presents for you," he said, "but first you must say 'how do you do' to this very distinguished and important guest who honours my poor house with his gracious presence."

By this time Nadina had reached the bottom of the stairs.

She walked a little way towards Nannk Osman, knowing she should have kept the child under control. She saw the man standing behind him.

He was a large, rather portly Turk with a beard, wearing the inevitable red fez.

It struck her that she had seen him before.

Suddenly she realised he was the Grand Vizier.

Next to the Sultan, the Grand Vizier was the most important man in Turkey.

She stood still.

She wondered if she should approach Nannk Osman to collect Rahmi from him or wait until he gave her the order.

It was then the Grand Vizier noticed her and said to his host:

"And who is this young woman?"

He was, of course, speaking in Turkish, and Nannk Osman replied:

"She is French—*Mademoiselle* Revon—and she is teaching my daughter languages, starting with her own."

Because he was speaking about her, Nadina thought it right to make a small curtsy.

Then the Grand Vizier walked a few steps nearer to her to say:

"You like being in Turkey? Are you happy here?"

"Very happy," Nadina replied, "and my pupil is very intelligent and clever, like her father."

She knew by the expression on Nannk Osman's face that she had said the right thing.

He was delighted to hear her praise him.

"You speak good Turkish, *Mademoiselle*," the Grand Vizier said.

"I thank you, Honourable Sir, for your kindness in saying so," Nadina replied.

She knew he was speaking the truth.

In fact, her Turkish was extremely good.

Her father had always taught her the language of every country they visited.

He insisted she should speak them fluently.

She should also know the right phrases to use.

They were more important than the actual words themselves.

Nannk Osman put the child into her arms.

With Rahmi screaming that she wanted to be with him, he took the Grand Vizier into his most spectacular Sitting-Room.

It was certainly impressive.

The furniture was carved and gilded and a huge crystal chandelier hung from the ceiling.

As they left the Hall, Nadina was aware that the Grand Vizier looked back at her.

There was no doubt of the admiring expression in his dark eyes.

She took Rahmi upstairs.

She was thinking as she went that it was fortunate that Nannk Osman was not annoyed at the child running so unconventionally to meet him.

It was something his wives would never do.

In fact, they would be forbidden to appear until they were sent for, or until he visited them.

"I must not let it happen again," Nadina told herself.

She knew, however, that her employer had been in a very good temper.

He was delighted to be entertaining the Grand Vizier.

He was ambitious and determined to make himself not only richer than he already was, but also more important.

She supposed that the height of his ambition

would be to become a Pasha.

She was certain that he had bribed a great number of the Ministers and those in authority in order to reach the position he was in now.

She wondered what new thing he was thinking of importing from Europe.

Alternatively, perhaps he was exporting something different.

Either way, it would benefit the Exchequer of Turkey.

She was aware that at the moment, like everything in the country, the economy was in a bad state.

How could it be anything else with the Sultan behaving as he was?

Only that morning a servant had regaled her with the latest information from the Royal Palace.

"The Sultan," he said, "plays with cocks and hens in the grandiose splendour of the gilded Reception Rooms."

He was laughing as he went on:

"The officials must remain expressionless as the Sultan chases the fluttering birds from room to room, and what do you think happens when he catches them?"

"I have no idea," Nadina replied.

"He hangs the Ottoman Empire's most prestigious medal for gallantry round their necks!" the servant chuckled. "And the Palace servants have to make certain that no cock or hen ever appears again without the Order."

It was mad. Of course it was mad!

Nadina, however, knew it would be a mistake to

comment, and so she said nothing.

What she had heard from Nannk Osman's wives was that Abdul Aziz had a favourite slave.

She was a sixteen-year-old Caucasian called Mihri Hanoum.

He spent every night and much of the day with her.

Rahmi's mother had lowered her voice as she related:

"The Sultan has given Mihri money. Much, much money!"

She mentioned a sum which Nadina calculated was the equivalent of one million pounds.

It seemed incredible.

And yet the stories coming from the Royal Palace were all the same.

Sometimes the Sultan forced his Courtiers to grovel on their knees and to kiss his feet before addressing him.

The whole business of the Government was brought to a halt because the Sultan refused to read anything written in ordinary ink.

He insisted that every paper brought to him was to be copied in red.

Bearing in mind that most of the stories were mainly servants' gossip, Nadina wondered what would happen in the future, a future which, of course, included herself.

She had felt safe in Turkey, but now she was not so sure.

She was also aware that Russian spies were filtering in.

They were too clever to let the Turks realise how dangerous they could be.

She was suddenly afraid that she might have to leave.

She was not certain where she would go, alone, without her Father and Mother.

Also she had no money.

She was saving every coin she received from Nannk Osman.

But he was a businessman and not known for his generosity.

She knew in his heart he considered that having a roof over her head and food to eat was payment in itself.

He gave her, somewhat grudgingly every month, a little Turkish currency.

She was, however, aware that it would buy practically nothing outside the country.

Anyway, she had no time to think about that at the moment.

She played with Rahmi, who was behaving a little petulantly because she wanted to be with her Father.

"Presents for Rahmi," she kept saying.

Nadina hoped that the Grand Vizier would not stay too long.

She knew that then Nannk Osman would want to be with his daughter.

It was, in fact, two hours before he left.

When Nannk Osman finally came upstairs with the presents for his daughter, Rahmi was thrilled with them.

She sat on her Father's knee, opening them one after another.

But she was very tired and, when Nannk Osman became aware of it, he said to Nadina:

"She must go to bed. I will be here to-morrow and she will be able to be with me most of the time."

"That is something she will certainly enjoy," Nadina replied. "She is tired now, but to-morrow she will recite a little poem she has been learning in French, which I hope will please you."

Nannk Osman smiled.

"It will please me very much," he replied.

He kissed his daughter and, as he rose to his feet, he said:

"The Grand Vizier was very interested in you, *Mademoiselle*. He thought it very clever of me to have my daughter taught French while she is still so young."

"That is the best time," Nadina replied, "and in a few years she will be as fluent as any French child. Then we will start Italian, or any other language you wish her to learn."

She hoped, as she spoke, that she would still be here.

Yet she was doubtful.

When Nannk Osman went away, she went to her own room.

She hoped to have a little time to herself in which to read before she joined the other women in the house.

Because they were uneducated, they never read a newspaper or a book.

She found it difficult to have very much in common with them.

All they really thought about was decking them-selves out in new clothes and new jewellery with which they would please their Lord and Master.

It was difficult for Nadina to find enough to read.

Nannk Osman was not a man who had much time for reading with the exception of the Financial Reports from the business, or books concerning trade.

Yet in his house in the City there were a large number of books.

They were, it was true, old and out-of-date. Nevertheless, Nadina found them interesting.

She had managed to persuade the servants to bring a number of them to the house to which they had now moved for the Summer.

She was, in fact reading a History Book on Egypt.

Although it was written in Arabic, she understood it.

She had been in Egypt with her Father and could speak and read that language.

She was reading about the appalling atrocities perpetrated by Mehemet Ali.

This was during the time when Britain was challenging Napoleon.

The son of an Albanian Moslem fisherman, he had earlier been saved from drowning in battle when he had been picked up in Nelson's barge.

He was a military genius who could not read or write, but boasted that he could read men's faces.

After the routing of Napoleon in Egypt, Mehemet Ali was employed by the Turkish Sultan to fight the British Forces.

He celebrated one victory by walking into Cairo through an avenue of British heads stuck on sticks.

His most famous action was to invite five-hundred leaders of a revolutionary band to an enormous supper in the Citadel of Cairo.

As his guests finished the excellent meal, Mehemet Ali ordered the doors to be locked.

Every guest, except one who managed to escape, was murdered.

This was one of the stories that Nadina found in Nannk Osman's Library.

It made her aware even more than she was aware at the moment that the Turks were excellent fighters but very cruel.

Each story made her more frightened than she was already.

However, she forced herself to think calmly.

She prayed over and over again that as a French Teacher to a Moslem child she was too unimportant to be in any real danger.

On the following day, to Rahmi's disappointment, her father could spend only very little time with her.

He had been summoned into the City.

"I will be as quick as I can," Nannk Osman promised.

Rahmi had to be content with that.

He was in a good humour.

Nadina thought he must be organising a very large order which would put more money into his pocket.

She already knew that the only thing he really cared about besides his business was his small daughter.

It was a touching weak-spot in what she often thought was a man made of iron.

Rather, perhaps "gold" was a better description!

Nannk Osman came back in the afternoon.

He immediately went for a swim in the Bosporus.

After it, he entered his comfortable cabin in the garden for a *siesta*.

Rahmi, hearing of her father's return, wanted to be with him.

But it was not until the sun had lost a little of its strength that he sent for her.

He played with his daughter for an hour before he sent for Nadina to fetch her.

They were still in the garden, and when she arrived Nannk Osman said:

"Put the child to bed, then I want to speak to you in my Sitting-Room."

"I will not be long," Nadina answered.

She took Rahmi upstairs, undressed her, washed her, and put her to bed.

When she kissed her good-night, Rahmi flung her arms round her neck.

"I love you, *M'mselle*," she said. "I love you!"

"And I love you," Nadina answered. "Now, go to sleep and to-morrow your father will play with you again."

"You tell me a story?" Rahmi begged.

"I will tell you a story if you will tell me one," Nadina replied.

The little girl giggled.

"Rahmi tell very short story," she said, "you tell very long one."

"We will see about that," Nadina answered.

She thought with a smile that the child was growing like her father—ready to bargain on anything, but always to her own advantage!

Nadina went to the mirror to tidy her hair, then went downstairs.

A servant told her to her surprise that his Master was not, as she expected, in the small Study-like room in which he worked, but in the Drawing-Room.

She walked in.

He was sitting almost as if he were the Sultan himself, in the most important arm-chair in the centre of the room.

She curtsied and walked towards him, aware that he was watching her.

She thought there was a strange expression in his eyes.

As she reached him he said:

"Sit down, *Mademoiselle*. I have something to tell you."

Nadina obeyed him.

For the first time, she felt a little apprehensive as to what he was going to say.

She could not believe that he wished to dispense with her services.

She knew how pleased he was at the amount of French Rahmi had learnt.

There was silence.

Then Nannk Osman said:

"When the Grand Vizier came here yesterday and saw you, he sent for me to-day because he wanted to speak to me about you."

"About me?" Nadina asked in surprise. "But, why? What . . . did he . . . say?"

She had a sudden fear that the Grand Vizier wanted her to teach his children.

She was very happy where she was and she loved Rahmi.

She had no wish to leave, even though it would

be to the household of the Grand Vizier.

"The Grand Vizier intimated to me this afternoon," Nannk Osman went on, "that he wished you to become his wife."

The words seemed to Nadina to vibrate round the room.

It was almost as if they were intoned.

She stared at her employer as if she could not believe what she had heard.

Then she said in a voice that did not sound like her own:

"Did you say . . . he wants . . . me to be . . . his w-wife?"

"That is what he told me," Nannk Osman said, "and, of course, it is a very great honour."

"B-but . . . he is married . . . he has a wife!" Nadina stammered.

Nannk Osman smiled.

"The Grand Vizier is, of course, a Moslem and may take four wives. At the moment he has only two and you would be his third."

"But . . . I am a . . . Christian!" Nadina protested.

Nannk Osman smiled again.

"So was the French Sultana," he said.

"I . . . I do not believe it!" Nadina gasped. "He cannot have suggested anything so . . . so . . ."

She stopped, knowing that what she had been about to say would be interpreted as insulting.

"It is a very great honour!" Nannk Osman repeated.

chapter three

ONE thing Nadina had learnt when she was travelling with her father was self-control.

With the greatest difficulty she kept her voice quiet and low as she said:

"You must understand that as a Christian and indeed a Frenchwoman, I have no wish to marry a Moslem."

Nannk Osman stared at her.

She realised he was genuinely surprised by her reply.

"I do not think you understand," he said. "The Grand Vizier could ask for you to be one of his Concubines. Instead, he has done you the greatest honour of inviting you to be his wife."

"His *third* wife!" Nadina said quietly.

"Who knows?" Nannk Osman said. "In time he may make you his chief wife."

There was silence before the Turk went on:

"I know what is in his mind at this very difficult

time. He believes that because you resemble Aimée Dubucq de Rivery, you might play the same part as she did in the history of our country."

Nadina looked at him questioningly, then she understood.

There was no one in the whole of Turkey who did not know the amazing story of the French Sultana.

At the end of the last century the Algerian Corsairs captured a French girl in the Mediterranean.

She was leaving School in France to return to Martinique, where she had been born.

Because she was so attractive, they gave her as a present to the Sultan of Turkey, Abdul Hamid I.

He was a fifty-nine-year-old voluptuary, bored with life.

He had a great number of Concubines who no longer interested him.

Aimée was intelligent enough to realise that, having once been captured, there was no escape.

She was put through the Academy of Love and waited for the summons to the Sultan's bed.

When it came, he was astonished by her beauty and also by her brain.

It was then the French girl set out to capture him not only with her body but with her intelligence.

Abdul Hamid, who had been Sultan for eleven years, was rejuvenated.

When she presented him with a son, he made Aimée's position secure.

As Nasha—"The Beautiful One"—she became his unquestionable favourite.

Her influence began to be shown not only in the Palace, but also outside it.

When Abdul Hamid died, she ingratiated herself

with his son and heir, Selim.

They became very close to each other, for he found it impossible to run the country without her help.

A "New Army" was founded, loyal only to Selim and disciplined on French lines.

French engineers started a cannon factory.

French military manuals were translated into Turkish.

Turkey's first weekly newspaper appeared—*Le Moniteur de l'Orient*.

It was inevitable that Aimée's relationship to Selim was questioned.

She was a full-blooded Frenchwoman in the prime of life consigned through her husband's death to chastity.

Selim was uninterested in his Harem and died childless.

The gossips whispered that they had become lovers.

Those who intrigued in the Palace pointed out that Selim was the only person in the way of the accession of Aimée's son.

They expected her to plot against him.

But both the inside and outside world knew of Aimée's selfless influence on the young Sultan.

There was great trouble during his reign.

Turkey was attacked by the French, but Selim made history by, on Aimée's advice, appointing the first Turkish Ambassador to France.

Finally, Selim was forced to resign by the Janissaries, who had become over-powerful.

His half-brother, Mustapha, was the heir to the throne, but he did not last long.

After a violent revolt Mahmud, Aimée's son, became Sovereign and reigned for thirty-one years.

He earned the title of "The Reformer."

The reforms which were desperately needed were entirely due to his mother's influence.

When finally Aimée, the Queen Mother, died, she had become a figure of admiration to the whole world.

Her power, and the inspiration she had given to three Sultans, became a legend in Turkish history.

There was no one who did not speak of the little French girl from Martinique with reverence.

The story flashed through Nadina's mind.

Although she had not thought of it before, she remembered reading that Aimée was golden-haired, as she was.

She, too, had a pointed face which was dominated by two huge blue eyes.

The French girl also, according to Historians, had a perfectly-formed Cupid's-bow of a mouth.

Because she was intelligent, Nadina could understand the reasoning behind the Grand Vizier's need of her.

But she could not think of anything more terrible than being incarcerated in his Palace, and to be touched by him as his wife.

Despite their long travels to a great many parts of the world, her Father had ensured that Nadina was very innocent.

Men had, of course, admired her ever since she had been a child.

Yet they were too frightened to approach her in any way.

Her Father had taken care to keep both her and

her Mother, who was very beautiful, out of sight.

All Nadina could think now was that somehow she must save herself.

Because she was silent, Nannk Osman took her agreement for granted.

"The Grand Vizier," he said, "is busy to-day and to-morrow. But he will come here the day after. Then he will make plans for your marriage."

He sighed.

"Little Rahmi will miss you," he said, "but somehow I must arrange for her to go on with her French lessons. If I give her many presents, we must hope in time she will forget you."

He smiled slightly before he added:

"As I said to the Grand Vizier, I am deeply gratified that I should have in my house a woman whom he desires."

The satisfaction in his voice made Nadina feel as if the prison gates were already closing on her.

She wanted to scream, but still in a controlled voice she said quietly:

"You will understand, Master, that this has been a shock! I would like time to think about it, although I appreciate what you are saying!"

"Of course, of course!" Nannk Osman agreed. "But when the Grand Vizier comes here on Wednesday, please him in the way that every woman should please a man."

He spoke sharply.

He sensed the rebellion within her even though she had not spoken of her feelings.

With dignity Nadina rose and, holding her head high, said quietly:

"I wish to retire, Master."

She curtsied.

"Go!" he said. "And we will celebrate this happy occasion. I will order a feast for the Grand Vizier when he arrives which will show him better than any words how much I appreciate his patronage."

Nadina felt she could not bear to hear any more.

She went from the room and ran up the stairs to her own bed-room.

There she lay flat on her bed.

She was not crying, as any other woman might have done, but thinking.

Then she was praying to her Father.

Speaking to him as she had done ever since she had lost him, she said:

"Help me, Papa . . . help me! What would . . . you do in the . . . position I am in . . . now?"

She had seen her Father in action so often.

They had moved from one country to another, hiding and living always with the fear that their disguise had been penetrated and their enemies had found them.

There had been times when at any second they might have been exposed.

And yet, Nadina thought, they had survived and been ecstatically happy.

"Help me, Papa . . . help me," she prayed again.

Then she knew the answer.

*　　*　　*

The next morning Nannk Osman left the house for the City.

As soon as he had gone, Nadina informed the Chief Servant that she wished to go shopping.

46

This was nothing unusual.

He merely asked her what time she required a carriage.

She replied that she would leave immediately after the midday meal.

While Rahmi had her *siesta* she could be with her Mother.

Nadina ate with the two wives and their sons.

She then asked Rahmi's Mother if she would take care of her daughter.

"If you are going shopping, why are you going so early?" the woman asked. "I would have come with you, as I need some new clothes."

This was something Nadina had already anticipated.

She had for that reason chosen to go immediately after luncheon.

The Turkish women would want to sleep and would consider it too hot to move about.

Nadina excused herself from the Dining-Room.

She put on her *yashmak* and the disguising *burnouse* which covered her from head to foot.

It made her, she always thought, completely inconspicuous.

She might be eighteen or eighty.

She knew there would be none of the side-long glances from men.

These were inevitable if she went to the shops or the Bazaar dressed as a European.

She drove in a comfortable carriage drawn by two horses into the City.

There she told the coachman to take her to the shop which she knew was nearest to the British Embassy.

The horses came to a standstill outside a shop which was large enough to have its products on several floors.

"Wait for me here," Nadina said. "I have a great many things to buy and I will be a long time."

The coachman grunted a reply.

She guessed he would sleep comfortably in her absence.

He would not therefore be particularly interested in how long she kept him waiting.

She went into the shop in which she had often been before.

Walking past the counters on the Ground Floor, she found herself at the back of the building.

She felt certain there would be another entrance and was not disappointed.

There was a door going out into a dirty courtyard through which she could reach a narrow lane.

It was little more than a passage.

This took her back into the main thoroughfare.

It was only a short distance to the British Embassy.

A large building, it stood in a garden with the Union Jack flying outside the main gate.

There were sentries on either side of the front door.

Tentatively, Nadina asked for Mr. Lyle Westley.

As she spoke his name, she was for a moment desperately afraid in case he had already left.

"Is Mr. Westley expecting you?" a servant asked.

"No, but tell him that *Mademoiselle* Nadina Revon wishes to see him."

As she spoke, Nadina removed her *yashmak*.

The covering over her hair fell back.

The servant looked surprised, but he said nothing.

He showed her into a Waiting-Room and, as there was nobody else there, Nadina was able to remove the *burnouse*.

When the servant returned, she appeared very different from how she had looked before.

She was wearing a pretty muslin gown, the colour of her eyes.

She might easily, she thought when she glanced in the mirror, have come from the Rue de la Paix.

Instead, it was from a Moslem house, where she had been told it was a great honour to be the third wife of the Grand Vizier!

"Will you come this way, *Mademoiselle*?" the servant asked.

She followed him down the passage and he opened a door.

In a comfortable Sitting-Room which was furnished in English style there was Lyle Westley.

Nadina was so relieved to see him that she gave a little cry of delight.

She almost ran across the room towards him.

He, too, was looking very different from the way he had looked when he had escaped in Nannk Osman's clothes.

He seemed younger and undoubtedly more English, besides being a very handsome man.

He held out his hand.

"This is a surprise, *Mademoiselle*!" he exclaimed. "I am delighted to see you!"

"I have come to you for help," Nadina answered. "Although I hate to impose on you, there is no one else to whom I can turn."

"You know that after what you did for me," Lyle Westley replied, "I am deeply in your debt, and of course I will help you in any way I can."

He thought the smile that lit up her face was very becoming.

Nadina sat down on the chair he indicated.

As she did so, Lyle Westley knew he had not been mistaken in thinking that she was one of the loveliest women he had ever seen.

After the dark-skinned Turkish women who thronged the streets and the women he had seen in Russia, Nadina looked like a flower in an English garden.

Then he told himself that he was forgetting—she was not English, but French.

It was unusual for a French girl, unless she came from Normandy, to have such vivid blue eyes.

He seated himself opposite her before he asked:

"Now, tell me—what is the trouble?"

"I have to leave Turkey immediately!" Nadina replied.

Lyle Westley raised his eye-brows.

"Immediately? But why? I thought when I first heard you singing in my language that you sounded happy."

"I was," Nadina agreed, "but . . . something has happened and I have to get away."

"Where do you want to go to?" Lyle Westley asked.

Nadina drew in her breath.

Then, looking at him as if to watch his reaction, she said quietly:

"To England . . . I must go to England because there I will be . . . safe."

Lyle Westley raised his eye-brows.

"England?" he queried. "Why not France?"

"Because . . . I am . . . English."

Now he stared at her in astonishment.

"English!" he exclaimed. "Then why are you posing as a Frenchwoman when, as you know, the English have been accepted in Turkey since the Crimean War made the Turks our allies."

"Yes, I know that," Nadina said, "but it was . . . safer for me to . . . pretend to be . . . French."

Lyle Westley looked puzzled.

"Safer? I do not understand."

There was silence until Nadina whispered:

"Perhaps it is a . . . mistake to let you know . . . too much . . . but if you could just . . . help me to . . . get to England . . . I have no money . . . that is . . . all I am . . . asking."

Lyle Westley sat back in his chair.

"There are many reasons why you should trust me and tell me a little more. For anyone as young and as beautiful as you, it would not be easy to travel to England without a chaperon, and, of course, I feel responsible for you."

He knew as he spoke that Nadina was debating with herself whether or not she should tell him the truth.

He found this curious and at the same time amusing.

He was used to people trusting him with their secrets without any prevarications.

And yet this young girl was weighing up his qualities.

Watching her, his eyes on her face, he waited.

Finally Nadina said:

"My Father always said it was a great mistake to trust anyone and it might—if there was trouble—be best for you to know as . . . little as . . . possible about . . . me."

Lyle Westley was astonished.

It seemed impossible that this pretty girl should have secrets of any importance.

Anyhow, why should they in any way affect him?

He himself was used to trusting no one, not even, as he had once said, his own shadow.

Therefore, he merely said:

"I understand exactly what you are feeling. At the same time, I think, before I sponsor your application, you must tell me at least of whom you are afraid."

"Very well," Nadina said. "The Grand Vizier has asked for me to be his . . . third wife!"

She spoke in a low voice and her eyes did not meet his.

"The Grand Vizier?" Lyle Westley exclaimed. "It cannot be true."

"He came to the house yesterday," Nadina explained, "and my employer, Nannk Osman, considered it a very great honour that he should wish me to be . . . his wife."

"You are—quite sure that is what he intends?" Lyle Westley enquired.

"He thinks because I am French and because I have fair hair I am like Aimée Dubucq de Rivery," Nadina explained.

There was no need to say any more.

Lyle Westley knew the story of Aimée as well as he knew the tale of "Cinderella."

He was also aware of the Sultan's peculiarities and could follow the Grand Vizier's reasoning.

This was apart from the fact that Nadina was exceedingly desirable as a woman.

Aloud he said:

"And you would not think of accepting such a high position in Turkey?"

"I would rather . . . die!" Nadina said sharply. "And as I am English I must go to my own country although I have never been there."

"Why not?"

There was a pause before she said, as if reluctantly:

"M-my Father could not . . . return for reasons of his own."

Lyle Westley bent forward.

"Will you tell me now your Father's name?" he asked.

Again there was a pause before Nadina replied:

"Richard Talbort."

If she had thrown a bomb into the middle of the room, Lyle Westley could not have been more astonished.

He sat up straight.

In a voice of sheer incredulity he repeated:

"Richard Talbort? Can you possibly mean the Diplomat?"

"Yes . . . he was . . . my Father."

To say that Lyle Westley was astonished was to put it mildly.

No one who had ever had anything to do with the Diplomatic Service or the ministry of State for Foreign Affairs could be unaware that Richard Talbort was the most wanted man in the world.

A brilliant young Diplomat, he had in 1854 gone to the Russian Court of Nicholas I.

Almost as soon as he arrived, he fell in love with one of the Tsar's nieces, the Princess Olga.

Tsar Nicholas was a cruel despot. He was busy marrying Olga to a Prince of the Royal Blood.

He was debauched and old, but extremely rich.

Richard Talbort was exceedingly handsome and also a very charming man.

Princess Olga said later that she fell in love with him the moment she met him.

Just before her marriage was to be announced, approved by all the Tsar's older relatives, Richard Talbort and Princess Olga ran away.

They left Russia, pursued on the Tsar's orders by the Third Section, with instructions to kill Talbort on sight.

They were to bring Princess Olga back to St. Petersburg.

Wildly, ecstatically happy as few people are privileged to be, Olga and Richard Talbort fled from country to country.

The Russians pursued them wherever they went.

Yet because Richard was an extremely astute and clever man, he had an acute sense of danger.

He also, wherever he stayed, made friends, who were only too willing to outwit the Russians.

As a nation, Russia was very heartily disliked almost everywhere.

Sometimes they stayed for a long time before they were forced to move on.

Three years after their marriage, when they were in India, Nadina was born.

Her birth only made Richard and Olga's love for

each other deeper because she was a part of it.

Nadina could never remember a time when her Father and Mother were not talking to each other with love in their eyes.

The whole world seemed to be illuminated with sunshine because they were so happy.

There were moments of fear, moments when Richard Talbort's intuition told him it was time to move on.

Then they would hurry away.

Sometimes there was only an hour to spare before the place in which they were living was discovered by the Russians.

Whether or not they lay awake worrying about the future, Nadina had been perfectly happy to be with them, to be loved and cossetted by them both.

To her, the endless movement and travel was just amusing.

There were new things to play with and different children about whose languages she quickly learnt.

Richard Talbort had a genius for languages—especially oriental ones.

It was one of the reasons he had been sent to Russia.

Only French was spoken at the Royal Court.

He could talk to the servants in the Palace and the serfs in the fields.

It was just as he talked to the Indians in Urdu and to the inhabitants of Burma, Java, and Ceylon in their own languages.

They visited many other countries.

They moved on only when it was absolutely necessary.

The years passed quickly.

And yet Richard and Olga's love for each other seemed to increase rather than diminish.

Nadina was eighteen when disaster overcame them.

They arrived in the South of Turkey, having spent a particularly happy time in getting there.

Sadly Olga contracted one of the terrible fevers that are always to be found in that part of the world.

She fought against it.

Although Richard knew that danger was approaching, he could not move her.

He was then informed that the Russians were coming nearer.

He knew, as he could not carry Olga to safety, what he must do.

First, he told Nadina of his plans.

"You must go to Constantinople as a French-woman, then try somehow to get to England."

He paused before he said:

"I am sure the family will have forgotten me by now, my darling, and they will welcome you. In any case, there is still money in the Bank which you can obtain when you prove yourself to be my daughter."

He had always been able to make their journeys as comfortable as possible because he was a rich man.

What was more, Olga had brought with her jewellery and also a great deal of the magnificent gems which belonged to her family.

They were easy to sell.

It was unfortunate at this moment that the

medicines the Doctors had prescribed for Nadina's Mother had been paid for with the jewels.

The fever that burned in Olga's body could not be stemmed.

Because Nadina was her Father's daughter, she obeyed him and did exactly as he told her.

He gave her every penny he possessed which was at that time not very much.

He had intended to withdraw money from the Bank when he reached Constantinople.

He found a man and his wife who he knew he could trust.

He sent Nadina away with them at night, hoping the Russians would not see them go.

Only as she was saying good-bye to him did Nadina ask:

"What about . . . you . . . Papa? How can I . . . leave you . . . here?"

"You have to go, my precious," he answered, "and you know that I must stay with your Mother."

"But . . . the Russians may . . . kill you."

He shook his head.

"I will not allow them to do that. I know now that my beloved wife will never recover, and when she leaves this life I intend to join her. We will wake up together in Paradise, or whichever Kingdom of the Gods will have us."

He spoke as if it were something happy he was about to do, an adventure to go on like so many of their other adventures.

Despite the dangers, they had all enjoyed them.

They laughed when they eluded their pursuers as if it were a great joke.

Nadina had not cried at the time.

Her Father held her closely to him as if he could not bear to let her go.

Then he said:

"God bless you, my darling. You know that your Mother and I will be helping and guiding you. And always remember, I have been the happiest and luckiest man in the whole world!"

Nadina knew that was true.

He had waved her off with the couple who were taking her to Constantinople.

Then he had gone back into the house.

He took the poison he had kept ready in case they had been caught by the Third Section.

He gave his wife the same potion.

As she drove away, Nadina knew that when the Russians did arrive, they would find her Father and Mother locked in each other's arms.

They would be looking ecstatically happy.

As her Father had said, they had gone to Paradise together.

Now she knew her Father was guiding her. It would be wise to tell Lyle Westley the truth.

She therefore told him exactly what had happened.

Because of the life he lived, she knew he would understand.

To Lyle Westley it was a revelation.

Yet it was just what he had expected of Richard Talbort.

There had been reports of him from time to time reaching the British Embassy in the various countries in which Lyle Westley had stayed.

Richard Talbort had gradually become a legend

among young Diplomats, especially those going to St. Petersburg.

"Do your best to keep us in touch with what is happening," the Secretary of State for Foreign Affairs would say before they left London, "and for God's sake, do not lose your heart as Richard Talbort did!"

The young man in question usually laughed.

"I will do my best not to, Sir" was the reply.

There was no doubt that the tale of Richard Talbort and Princess Olga, and their journeys over the world, lost nothing in the telling.

As Nadina had anticipated, the end was just as her Father had planned.

The Russians had burst in early the next morning after she had gone.

They found Richard and his wife in each other's arms, apparently asleep.

Because they were dead, it was impossible for the Russians to do anything but report to St. Petersburg that their mission was at an end.

That was, as far as the two main characters were concerned.

However, their daughter had disappeared.

Richard Talbort had warned Nadina that until she reached England she must be disguised.

"Tell no one who you really are," he said. "As you speak fluent French, you will be welcomed in Constantinople. However, do not linger in Turkey, but get to England as quickly as you can."

"I will do my best, Papa," Nadina promised.

At the same time, she realised it was going to be difficult without him to fend for herself.

Even Richard Talbort did not realise how

completely he had dominated his wife and daughter.

It was he who had decided where they should go, where they should stay, and what they should do.

There were no arguments.

For the first time in her life, Nadina was alone.

The old couple who had taken her to Constantinople were very kindly.

When she told them she was prepared to teach French to children, they approached one of their relatives.

He found her a position with Nannk Osman.

It had been as easy as that.

Nadina had very little money.

She felt it would be too dangerous to go to the Bank and claim what her Father had deposited there.

She was sure it was a large sum, as they had been so short of money on their last journey.

But, if the Russians were looking for her, they would undoubtedly expect her to visit the Bank.

They would be waiting.

Her eighteen years had taught her about Russian tenacity.

They disliked being beaten at anything they undertook.

The members of the Third Section would not be pleased at having to report to St. Petersburg that their quarry had evaded them.

It would therefore be a coup if they could take back a prisoner, especially if it was Richard Talbort's daughter.

"You do see," Nadina was saying, "that I have not dared to go to the Bank, even though I am sure Papa has a great deal of money there."

"You are absolutely right not to do so," Lyle Westley agreed. "I am finding it hard to believe, however, that after all these years I am actually looking at the daughter of the man I admire perhaps more than anybody else."

Nadina smiled, and it made her look very beautiful.

"I like to hear you say that," she said, "as I have never thought that Papa wasted his brain or his brilliance. Could it be a waste to be so happy and to make my Mother and me as happy as he was?"

"Of course not," Lyle Westley said quietly.

"What is more," Nadina went on, "they spread happiness to people wherever they went. It was as if they sent out vibrations of love, making people laugh because they were laughing. And I have never known Papa refuse to help anyone who was in trouble."

"I think he was a magnificent man!" Lyle Westley said. "And it makes me very proud to be able to help his daughter."

Nadina's eyes lit up.

"Then . . . you will . . . help me?"

"To the very best of my ability." Lyle Westley smiled.

As he spoke, he thought it was not going to be easy, but he did not say as much to Nadina.

What he had said made her happy.

She looked, he thought, like the sunshine as she smiled up at him with her Cupid's-bow lips.

Her eyes were shining like stars.

"What I am going to do now," he said, "is to consult with the Ambassador as to what would be the best and quickest way to get you to England. Meanwhile, I must leave you alone while you have a cup of coffee."

"Thank you . . . thank you!" Nadina cried. "I knew I was right when I felt that Papa was telling me to come to you!"

"Of course you were!" Lyle Westley agreed.

chapter four

LYLE Westley walked along the passage to the Ambassador's room.

When he opened the door he was glad to find that His Excellency was alone.

He looked up and exclaimed:

"Oh, there you are! I was just going to send for you. There is a cable come from England."

"For me?" Lyle Westley asked.

"About you," the Ambassador replied. "You are to go back immediately. Her Majesty the Queen wishes to see you."

Lyle Westley raised his eye-brows.

"I am not surprised," the Ambassador went on. "The Queen is far more astute than most of her Ministers and she has been suspicious of the Russians for some time."

Lyle Westley nodded because he knew this.

"When you informed the Earl of Derby," His Excellency continued, "that the Empress of Russia felt it was a religious crusade for the Balkan Christians to establish Constantinople as the greatest City in Christendom, I knew that bit of information would go straight to Windsor Castle."

"It all occurred," Lyle Westley said, "when the Empress was influenced by those two books published in Russia that I told you about."

"I had heard about them before," the Ambassador replied. "I was told they had triggered off a wave of militarism and did their best to start an uprising in the name of Christ against the Infidels."

"I only hope you have time to prevent it," Lyle Westley said, "now that you are warned."

"It is not going to be easy," the Ambassador sighed, "but you will be out of it and on your way to England, you lucky chap!"

Lyle Westley sat down on a chair opposite the Ambassador's desk.

"What I came to talk to you about," he said, "is a young woman who must leave for England immediately and who needs your help to do so."

"A young woman?" the Ambassador asked.

Then before Lyle Westley could reply he said:

"I have the idea that you are referring to the French Governess whom you told me saved your life two days ago."

"You are right," Lyle Westley replied, "but she is not French. She is the daughter of Richard Talbort."

The Ambassador stared at him.

"Did you say—Richard Talbort?" he asked.

"I did. It seems incredible, but before he took poison to prevent him and his wife falling into the hands of the Russians, he sent her away to

Constantinople and told her to pretend to be French."

The Ambassador drew in his breath but did not speak, and Lyle Westley went on:

"Some friends of Talbort's who brought her to the City found her the job of teaching the daughter of Nannk Osman. She has been safe there up until now."

"Do you mean—the Russians have found her?" the Ambassador asked.

Lyle Westley shook his head.

"No, not yet. But the Grand Vizier wishes to take her as his third wife!"

The Ambassador looked at Lyle Westley as if he had gone mad. Then he said:

"You must be joking!"

"Unfortunately, it is the truth," Lyle Westley replied. "You understand that we have to get her out of Constantinople before he starts to plan their marriage."

There was a moment's silence.

Then the Ambassador said:

"You said—'we.' Now, listen to me, Westley— in no circumstances whatsoever can the British Embassy become involved in this!"

Lyle Westley was still, but he did not reply and the Ambassador went on:

"You know the position I am in. With the information you have given me I have to try to get the Army mobilised and the Navy—and God knows there is little enough of it—into position to control the Bosporus. To whom can I turn for help?"

As he asked the question, he flung out his arms.

"There is only one person," be went on, "who has any sense in the whole administration, and that is the Grand Vizier!"

Lyle Westley could not argue.

He knew the Ambassador was speaking the truth.

"The Sultan is mad," the Ambassador continued, "but the Grand Vizier has a modicum of sense, and I will make him take some action, although, as you well know, with the whole country deeply in debt, it is going to be an almost impossible task."

As he finished speaking, the Ambassador got to his feet and walked across the room.

He stood at the window, looking blindly out at the flower-filled garden.

In a quiet voice Lyle Westley said:

"I understand your problem, Ambassador, but I have to help Nadina, not only because she saved my life but also because she is Richard Talbort's daughter."

"I understand—I understand your predicament," the Ambassador said sharply, "but I cannot offend the Grand Vizier at this particular moment."

"All right," Lyle Westley said, "I will have to manage on my own, and as I have to go back to England, I will take her with me."

The Ambassador turned round.

"There is one thing I forgot to tell you," he said. "The Prime Minister has sent a message to the nearest British Battleship to pick you up from whichever point you choose. You can inform the Captain from here where that will be."

Lyle Westley's eyes lightened.

Unexpectedly the Ambassador smiled.

"You are getting very grand!" he said. "If you ask me, when you do reach Her Majesty, she will elevate you to the House of Lords!"

He paused before he added:

"I am sorry I did not offer you my condolences sooner, but your Father died while you were away. You knew that, of course?"

Lyle Westley nodded his head.

"Yes, I heard about it when I was in St. Petersburg, but at that moment it was impossible for me to go home, as you will understand."

"Of course," the Ambassador said. "I suppose I should be using your title, and 'Sir Lyle' sounds very impressive."

"Damn being impressive!" Lyle Westley retorted. "What I am concerned about at the moment is saving my life and that of Nadina Talbort."

The Ambassador sat down again at his desk.

"I know that," he said, "and I will do everything I can to help, but it must be under the greatest secrecy and without the Grand Vizier even suspecting that the Embassy is involved."

Lyle Westley thought for a moment before he said:

"Even as we have been talking, an idea has come to me. All I need is money and some of your most trusted men who will not talk."

The Ambassador spread out his hands.

"You know you can have that," he said. "Forgive me, Westley, if I sound unsympathetic, but I feel as if we are sitting on a bomb which might at any moment blow us all sky-high!"

"I understand completely," Lyle Westley said. "I

realise, too, that the sooner we are out of your way, the better."

He walked out through the door, and as he did so he looked back.

With a twist of his lips he said:

"Thank you for small mercies. I am not ungrateful, but everything is more difficult when one is accompanied by a pretty young woman."

He left the room before the Ambassador could reply.

When he had gone, Walter Baring put his hand over his eyes.

He was thinking that never in his whole life in the diplomatic service had he known a more difficult and tangled situation than he was faced with at that particular moment.

* * *

Lyle Westley did not go directly back to the room where he had left Nadina.

Instead, he went up the stairs of the Embassy to the top floor, where there was a locked room.

It was known only to a few people.

Even most of those who lived in the Embassy were not aware of what it contained.

The key was kept in a special place for those who had access to it.

This meant that if someone was in a great hurry, they did not have to look for a particular person to unlock the door.

Lyle Westley found the key.

He made certain there was no one about, and opened the door.

The attic room was filled with wardrobes, chests-of-drawers, and cupboards.

Lyle Westley went straight to one wardrobe.

When he opened it, it was not, as might have been expected, full of clothes on racks.

Shelves had been inserted on which there were wigs.

There must have been at least twenty-five of them.

They were all propped up so that the hair, which had been very skilfully arranged, was not flattened.

Lyle Westley took a long time choosing which one he wanted.

Carrying it carefully so as not to make it untidy, he left the room.

He locked the door behind him and replaced the key in its hiding-place.

He covered the wig with his handkerchief and went downstairs.

Nadina was not sitting, as he expected, in a chair, but standing at the window, looking out into the garden.

She turned round quickly when he came in and said eagerly:

"You have been such a long time . . . I was beginning to think you had . . . forgotten about . . . me."

"I had not forgotten," Lyle Westley replied, "but things are more difficult than I expected."

He saw the expression of anxiety in her eyes, and said quickly:

"Do not worry. I will look after you. You are going to England, but I am coming with you."

"Coming with me?" Nadina repeated. "But of

course you must not do that! You have work to do here, and I am sure I can manage on my own."

"I will answer that by saying that I have no choice," Lyle Westley said. "Her Majesty the Queen has sent for me."

As he looked at Nadina, he knew she had been afraid of travelling to England alone.

Aloud she said:

"If I can . . . go with you . . . that . . . will be very . . . wonderful for me!"

"I only hope it will be," Lyle Westley warned, "but let me tell you that we have to be very clever about this. One mistake could land us both in the arms of the Russians."

"I know that," Nadina answered in a low voice, "but if Papa was able to defy them for twenty-one years, I feel sure you will get us both safely to England."

"All you have to do is to carry out my instructions very carefully," Lyle Westley said.

"You know I will do anything you tell me to do," Nadina replied positively.

"Very well then," Lyle Westley said, "this is the first thing you will need."

As he spoke he pulled his handkerchief off the wig he was holding in his hand.

For a moment Nadina stared at it in surprise.

Then she understood.

It was quite an attractive wig, made with hair that was a rather dull brown, the inconspicuous common hair colour of many Europeans.

Nadina did not take it from him, and after a moment Lyle Westley put it down on a table.

"Because it is urgent for you to get away," he

began, "we must leave to-night, and this is what you have to do. . . ."

* * *

Nadina drove back from the City.

When she arrived she collected Rahmi from her Mother and took her up to her own room.

It was a strange situation, she thought.

The wives of Nannk Osman lived in one part of the house and seldom left each other's company.

She, on the other hand, was housed with Rahmi in what was essentially his part.

He could see his daughter whenever he wished to do so.

Nadina was relieved to find, when she returned from the City, that her employer had not yet come home.

She had spent so long at the Embassy, she was afraid he might be there before her.

She had no wish to answer questions as to what she had been doing.

It would be a mistake, she knew, to underrate his intelligence.

She had appeared to acquiesce to the wishes of the Grand Vizier.

Yet her perception told her that Nannk Osman was not deceived.

She had said nothing, but she had the uncomfortable feeling that he could read her thoughts.

He had been aware that her whole body and mind was in revolt at such an idea.

She was praying as she had prayed all the way back from the City.

It was that Lyle Westley would succeed in taking her away and that they would both reach England in safety.

She would not have been her Father's daughter if she had not realised the difficulties.

Lyle Westley had told her that the Grand Vizier must not be suspicious.

Also, that the British Embassy was not in any way to be involved.

He had spoken frankly.

He told her that the information he had brought from Russia meant that it was imperative for the Turkish Army to be mobilised, not only to fight in Bulgaria, but perhaps in defence of Constantinople itself.

"I am telling you something," he said, "which I would never tell anyone else, because one false step on our part might endanger the position that England holds at the moment in Turkey."

Nadina answered:

"I do understand. It would be better for . . . me to . . . die than to . . . do that."

"You are not going to die," Lyle Westley said. "But we will have to use our intelligence every second of the day from this moment."

Having said that, he did not let her linger in the Embassy.

She put on her *yashmak* and her *burnouse* and he took her out through a side gate.

"It is obvious," he said, "that the Russians will be watching the front of the building."

"Do you mean they might be expecting to see you?" Nadina asked.

"They might, although I suspect it is something

they do anyway, just in case any visitor is of interest to the Head of the Third Section in St. Petersburg."

He therefore escorted Nadina to another gate.

It led into a side street which was seldom used, not even by the servants.

It was easy for her to find her way from there back to the shop.

She entered the door by which she had left it.

Lyle Westley did not go with her.

He merely watched her until she was out of sight, knowing she was safe disguised as a Moslem woman.

What was really perturbing him was whether she would be able to carry out his instructions.

Then he told himself that she had survived for eighteen years with her Father.

It was insulting of him to imagine she would fail in what by comparison was easy.

He hurried back to the Embassy.

Going to the Cable-Room, be requested a message to be sent to the ship which would be sent to wherever he desired it.

He chose a place at the end of the Dardanelles which opened into the Aegean Sea.

From there a ship would move quickly into the Mediterranean.

One blessing was that having a Battleship take him back to England meant that they would not be intercepted by Russian ships.

The great ambition of the Russians had always been to gain access to the Mediterranean.

It was something the British were determined they should not have.

Having sent off his request, Lyle Westley went to his room.

He had a great deal to plan and a great deal to organise before the journey.

He knew exactly who inside the Embassy he must contact for help.

* * *

Nadina put Rahmi to bed and told her a story.

It was one she particularly enjoyed because it was about a little girl very much like herself.

She had spent a happy time with her Father.

Because he was feeling guilty at taking Nadina away from her, Nannk Osman had brought her even more presents than he had given her the previous day.

"Your Father spoils you!" Nadina said when she went to fetch her at bed-time.

"Rahmi not spoil," the child replied. "Very good an' very clever. Papa say so."

"Yes, of course you are!" Nadina agreed.

She pulled the little girl close and kissed her.

In the short time in which she had been teaching Rahmi, she had grown to love the child.

"I shall miss her," she told herself.

She felt upset that she must make Rahmi unhappy when she had gone.

But she would have had to leave her anyway.

It was just a little sooner than if she had stayed and married the Grand Vizier.

Even to think of him made her shudder, and Rahmi asked:

"Why you shaking? You frightened?"

It was a clever question, and Nadina replied:

"I just felt the wind."

"There no wind!" Rahmi said scornfully. "Day very, very hot. Papa gone to bathe in the sea. Rahmi want to bathe."

"One day soon," Nadina answered.

She had been waiting for the overwhelming heat that occurred in the Summer before she taught the child to swim.

She wondered who would do that when she had gone.

Then she told herself to forget everything but the instructions given to her by Lyle Westley.

She told Rahmi two stories as a special treat.

When she had finished the second one, the child had her eyes almost closed.

Nadina kissed Rahmi very gently on both cheeks.

Then she pulled the sheets over her.

As she did so, she thought that perhaps one day she would have a child of her own to look after.

'It would make me very happy,' she thought.

Then she remembered she must first have a husband.

The idea of the Grand Vizier giving her a baby made her shiver again.

She hurried to her bed-room and began to get everything ready.

She had put the wig in a cupboard and locked the door.

She did not try it on because she was afraid that somebody might come in and see it.

When it was time for supper she went downstairs.

As she had expected, the two wives were

bedecked in the most elaborate and expensive clothes.

Both were covered with jewellery.

She had noticed that they never bothered to dress up when Nannk Osman was away.

When he was at home they spent hours painting their faces and arranging their hair.

Then appeared in fantastic costumes that were exceedingly glamorous.

Nadina thought it was a pity that Nannk Osman took so little interest in either of his wives.

She was aware that the one thing with which he was in love was his business.

He thought about it, talked about it, and, she suspected, dreamt about it.

His wives, hardly understanding a word of what he said, just listened to him dumbly.

They appeared as if they were entranced by what he was saying.

He had, however, since Nadina's arrival, talked to her.

She was wise enough to make no comments, criticisms, or suggestions.

If she did ask him a question, it was an intelligent one.

He had, therefore, a listener who helped him to clarify his own brain.

The food was good, especially the fish that came fresh from the Bosporus every morning.

Because they were Moslems, they drank only the fruit drink that was popular all over the country.

Nadina knew that Nannk Osman himself had made quite a fortune out of it in his shops.

To-night Nadina was thinking that after she left,

he would have to go back to talking to his wives.

He went into a long explanation of what he was planning in the future, listing the new provisions he was bringing in from Europe.

It was, in fact, interesting.

Nadina, however, had to force herself to concentrate on what he was saying.

All the time she was thinking that time was passing.

She must be ready to do what Lyle Westley had told her to do.

At last, when Nannk Osman was tired of his own voice and yawning, he went to his own bedroom.

Nadina was free to go to hers.

Politely she said good-night to his two wives and went upstairs.

She slept in a room that opened out of Rahmi's.

She took a last look at the child, who was fast asleep.

Then she went to her own room to wait until it was a few minutes to twelve.

She had told Lyle Westley that after their Master had gone to bed the servants on duty would sleep on the floor, where they were expected to be on guard.

"Be sure they do not see you!" he said sharply.

Nadina knew there was no chance of that.

At five minutes to twelve she left her room and started to walk very softly along the corridor.

She went down a side staircase and out of the house by a door which led directly into the garden.

She moved slowly, as her Father had taught her to do, so that her footsteps were not heard.

It would have been impossible for anyone, even nearby, to hear her open the door.

She left it open as Lyle Westley had instructed her to do.

She kept to the bushes, even though there was no one on that side of the house to see her.

At last she reached the place on the terrace where she had first seen Lyle Westley.

Once there, she took off her muslin robe and nightgown to put them down on the white stones.

Beside them she put her slippers.

Beneath her nightgown she was wearing a gown which, on Lyle Westley's instructions, was the most inconspicuous one she possessed.

"You must bring nothing with you," he had said, "nothing that would make the servants say that something was missing after you had gone."

"I understand," Nadina answered.

At the last moment before she left the house she had taken her wig out of the cupboard, where she had hidden it.

To her surprise, when she looked in the mirror she saw that it was quite an attractive shape.

Yet it seemed to change her whole appearance.

She had the idea that it made her look older.

Then she realised it was arranged in a style that would have been more suitable to a woman of over thirty.

However, she was not particularly concerned about her looks.

She was more worried about whether Lyle Westley would arrive as he had promised, and they could get away.

She had been waiting for perhaps two minutes when he appeared.

The *Caique* with six men at the oars came silently alongside the terrace.

The oarsmen nearest the land held the boat still.

Lyle Westley put out his hand to steady Nadina as she climbed aboard.

No one said a word.

As soon as she was seated beside him in the stern, the oarsmen pushed the boat out into the Bosporus.

They dipped their oars into the water.

Then they were moving swiftly away, down the Bosporus, with the stars twinkling on the water.

Once Nadina was seated beside him, the only movement Lyle Westley made was to produce a woollen shawl.

He placed it round her shoulders.

She was not cold except from feeling somewhat nervous, and her heart was beating quickly.

They drew away from the land.

Nadina thought triumphantly that she had got away without there being any interference.

It was, she thought, a clever idea of Lyle Westley's.

When the household rose to-morrow morning and found her missing, they would assume that she had gone swimming.

At dinner, when Nannk Osman was not talking, she had said that, as it was growing so hot, she was longing to swim.

She also added that she must soon start teaching Rahmi.

"It cold in sea," one of the wives said.

"Not really," Nadina had replied. "If you knew how hot it was in the City this afternoon, you would have wanted to bathe, even if the Bosporus was frozen!"

They had laughed at this, and Nannk Osman said:

"It was delightful when I bathed before supper and I think, *Mademoiselle*, it will be safe for Rahmi to go into the water to-morrow or the next day."

"I will not keep her in too long," Nadina replied, "but I have promised her that by the summer she will swim as well as you do!"

Nannk Osman had smiled at the compliment.

He could never have too many of them.

He really preferred them to be about his brain and his possessions rather than himself.

The rest of the time during supper he discussed business.

Nadina, however, was certain that to-morrow they would remember why, feeling the heat, she had bathed while everybody else was asleep.

She looked at Lyle Westley sitting beside her.

The starlight was on his face.

She thought, as she had before, how handsome he was.

He was, however, looking very serious.

He was obviously concerned that everything would go as smoothly as he wished.

She had the feeling he was glad when, moving swiftly, they were out of sight of the opening into the Black Sea.

It had not occurred to Nadina before.

Yet perhaps the Russians, having lost him, were still suspicious!

It was like them, she thought, never to give up.

They were persistent even when it appeared unlikely they would get any results.

Almost without realising what she was doing, she looked back over her shoulder.

There was no boat following them.

Only the stars were reflected in the darkness of the water.

Immediately ahead there were the lights of Constantinople.

As if Lyle Westley had already given them instructions, the oarsmen pulled away from the shore.

There were fishing smacks, boats of every sort, and *Caiques* moored in the port, a few moving close to the quays.

There was no one to notice them as they passed.

The oarsmen moved so swiftly that Nadina thought they might have wings.

On and on they went, and now at last the City was left far behind.

They moved nearer in shore.

There were a few cliffs but otherwise barren land without a sign of a house.

Nadina wanted to ask where they were going.

Yet because Lyle Westley had not spoken to her, she knew that he wished for silence.

Her Father had said to her once:

"Talking can be dangerous. A voice carries clearly, especially at night, and automatically commands attention."

When they were moving away from a place in a great hurry, neither she nor her Mother had said a word.

But they, Nadina thought, had no need for words.

Her Father and Mother were close to each other; they were touching each other.

She knew that their love vibrated between them.

They were so happy together that even the danger they were in was unimportant.

Suddenly she felt very lonely.

She was setting off with a man she had met only twice. She had left behind her clothes and her precious possessions, although there were very few of them, as well as a child she loved.

She had nothing else to love now.

There was no one in England, if she ever reached it, who would welcome her or be glad to see her.

She felt suddenly afraid—afraid of the silence in which they were travelling.

The darkness seemed oppressive now that there were no lights except for the stars.

The future was shrouded in mist and she could not anticipate it even to herself.

Without even thinking what she was doing, but behaving as if she were a child, she slipped her hand into Lyle Westley's.

She thought she must hold on to something.

He was human even though he sat beside her in silence.

His fingers, strong and warm, closed over hers.

It was very comforting.

chapter five

THE men rowed on, moving quickly and efficiently.

Nadina realised they must be specially picked oarsmen.

She wondered where they were going.

She knew, however, it would be a mistake to speak until Lyle Westley allowed her to do so.

After some time had passed, Nadina was aware that they were in one of the strong, swift currents for which the sea in these parts was notorious.

The oarsmen were resting the oars and letting the current carry the *Caique* more swiftly than they could row.

After a little while she began to feel tired.

It had been a long day.

She had been nervous when she went to the Embassy and even more nervous when she returned.

It would have been so easy for something to go wrong.

Perhaps it would be impossible to carry out Lyle Westley's instructions?

As they went on, she pulled the shawl more closely around her shoulders.

It was not cold.

At the same time, there was a breeze from the sea.

Because she was tired, she felt she needed the warmth of the shawl.

She wondered if she would have anything else to wear.

Then she was sure that Lyle Westley would have thought of everything.

She was puzzling as to where they were going, when she dozed off.

Her head instinctively fell onto Lyle Westley's shoulder.

He put his arm round her.

He knew better than anyone else would have done that she was suffering from the exhaustion which comes so easily to those who face danger.

Her body was light against his.

She seemed insubstantial and as if she were not human.

'She is too young to have to suffer like this!' he thought angrily.

He decided that if he was to continue with his present way of life, he would not marry.

He certainly would not have any children.

It was not fair to them.

Then he remembered belatedly that now that his Father was dead, his rightful place was at home.

He was sure there would be plenty to keep him occupied.

There was the house, the estate, and of course, the family.

His Father had been a great autocrat.

All the Westleys, and there were a great number of them, had looked to him for guidance and, of course, for help.

The Solicitors would have been unable to get in touch with him.

But he was sure they would be carrying on in the same way they had when his Father was alive.

The pensioners would have received their money and the people on the estate paid every Friday.

The house would be run exactly as it had always been, smoothly and faultlessly, by a number of servants who had been there for years.

It was the tradition, when anyone new was wanted, for them to come, if possible, from the village.

He was well aware it was considered a great privilege to be employed at the "Big House."

When he took his Father's place, all the familiar traditions would carry on as they always had.

It struck him, as if for the first time, that his life of adventure and danger was over.

How could he undertake another mission when he knew he should be at home?

There would be no-one there to cope with the day-to-day problems.

Difficult and dull, they would occur among those to whom he was related and those he employed.

For a moment he felt he could not bear it.

Then he remembered that the Russians were pursuing him.

It would be impossible for him to undertake again the type of mission he had just completed and come back alive.

The future seemed bleak and incredibly boring.

Then he told himself that as Sir Lyle Westley he would undoubtedly take up a number of appointments, both in the County as well as in London.

Besides, if the Ambassador was right, the Queen might decide to elevate him to the Peerage.

This would solve two problems.

One, it would be very much more difficult for the Russians to assassinate him, and secondly, he knew that his voice would be listened to in the House of Lords with attention.

It seemed strange that all these things should be passing through his mind at a time when he was aware that both he and Nadina were in deadly danger.

The Russian spies would, he thought, have guessed that he was hidden somewhere in the Embassy.

They might also have been aware of the way by which he had left it.

They would learn—of course they would—that Nadina was missing.

Their astute minds would associate her absence with the fact that they had lost him near Nannk Osman's house.

With a twist of his lips he decided there was no use him worrying about what he would do when he returned to England.

What he had to consider at the moment was how he and Nadina could get there alive.

Dawn came early.

Nadina opened her eyes and realised she was still in the *Caique*.

They were still moving rhythmically through the smooth water.

She was also aware that her head was on Lyle Westley's shoulder.

His arm was holding her close to him.

For a moment she had no wish to move.

There was a light on the horizon and the last stars were fading overhead.

Lyle Westley looked down at her.

"You have been asleep," he said, "and now we are nearly at our destination."

They were the first words he had spoken.

In a very small voice that seemed almost caught in her throat she replied:

"I—I am . . . sorry if I have . . . made you . . . uncomfortable."

"You have done nothing of the sort," he said, "and to sleep was the most sensible thing you could do."

She raised her head.

She saw by the width of the sea on either side of them they must be somewhere in the Sea of Marmara.

"Where are we going?" she whispered.

"Eventually to where both you and I belong," Lyle Westley answered, "but we have first to do a little travelling."

He was speaking in English.

Nadina knew that he did not wish to mention names in front of the oarsmen.

They were picked men, and they were trusted by the Ambassador.

But Lyle Westley had learnt to trust nobody unnecessarily.

He did not speak again.

Although Nadina thought she ought to move from the shelter of his arms, she did not do so.

She just watched the sun coming up over the horizon.

It was dazzlingly golden as it swept away the shadows of the night.

It seemed as if the whole world glistened.

Over an hour later, when the sun was moving up the sky, the *Caique* moved nearer to the shore.

There was not much sign of human habitation.

Finally they drew into a small bay.

Nadina thought it seemed an isolated place.

They beached the boat. Two of the men got into the water to hold it steady.

To Nadina's surprise, Lyle Westley picked her up in his arms.

He carried her carefully until he had stepped from the *Caique* onto the sand.

Then he set her down on her feet.

One of the oarsmen brought ashore two suit-cases.

Then, as Lyle Westley thanked the men in Turkish, Nadina saw him give them a large amount of money.

They smiled and wished him "Good Luck."

In the daylight Nadina could see they were very tall men, heavily-built, and with large muscles on their bare arms.

She was feeling a little dazed, partly from sleep and partly because the sun dazzled her eyes.

It was only when she watched Lyle Westley picking up the suit-cases that she stared at him in astonishment.

In the darkness of the night she had had no idea what he was wearing.

When he had put her down on the sand she had been interested in the *Caique* in which they had travelled.

She saw now he was wearing what appeared to be a cassock.

She looked at his face, then gave a little gasp.

He had parted his hair in the middle and it covered the sides of his forehead.

The cassock buttoned up at the front.

At his neck she had a glimpse of something white and what she thought, when she could see it more clearly, would be a cross.

He was, however, walking quickly towards the low cliffs which bordered the bay.

When he reached them he put down the suit-cases and looked back.

Instinctively Nadina did the same.

The oarsmen were now back in the *Caique,* moving as if they were floating out to sea.

"They will go somewhere where they can rest," Lyle Westley said as if she had asked the question. "They did a magnificent job in getting us here so swiftly, and we should be very grateful to them."

"I am . . . of course I am," Nadina replied, "but where are we going now?"

"We are going," Lyle Westley replied, "to Eceabat."

He saw it meant nothing to Nadina, and he added:

"If you know your geography, you are aware we have to pass through the Dardanelles to reach the coast of the Aegean Sea, which is where we will be able to join the Battleship."

"Of course, I did realise we would have to do that," Nadina said.

"Now—let me look at you," Lyle Westley asked.

She raised her face to his.

"The whole trouble," he said, "is that you are far too pretty to be the sister of a missionary."

"Is that what I am?" Nadina asked.

"We have been travelling in central Turkey. Now, after reporting what progress we have made to our Headquarters in Constantinople, we are on our way to Canakkale."

Nadina was listening intently as he said with a smile:

"Now we have to make you look a little more like a female Missionary who would help me with the children."

Nadina was aware that she was being instructed.

She waited apprehensively.

She had never failed her Father when they had had to disguise themselves.

It was, however, different when she was with a man she did not know at all well, also to whom, she was quite certain, she was an encumbrance.

Lyle Westley was opening one of the suit-cases.

When he lifted the lid Nadina realised it was hers.

She could see something that looked like a rather dull dress, and what might be a night-gown.

What Lyle Westley was taking from it was a hat.

It was a very ordinary, cheap hat which could have come from anywhere.

He pushed up the crown which had been flattened in the suit-case, and handed it to her.

She put it on carefully over her brown wig.

Then she looked at him, waiting for his approval.

He did not say so, but he thought, as she had placed it at the back of her head, that it haloed her face.

It made her, in fact, look lovelier than ever.

He took from her shoulders the woollen shawl she had worn during the night.

He placed it in the case and shut it.

He then opened the other case.

From that he took a black hat which was exactly the type worn by a missionary.

Then, putting his hand down inside the case, he produced a pair of spectacles.

"Put these on," he said. "They will not hurt your eyes because the glass is plain, but they may make you look more severe."

Nadina laughed.

"Is that how a Missionary should look?" she asked.

"All the lady Missionaries I have met on my travels," Lyle Westley replied, "are exceedingly dull spinsters of 'uncertain age' whose faces resemble the back of a cab!"

Nadina laughed.

"I am sorry, but I have no wish to look like that!" she objected.

"It would be impossible, however hard you tried," Lyle Westley said, "so we must just hope that no-one will notice you."

He picked up both the suit-cases, then asked:

"You have comfortable shoes in which to walk?"

"I hesitated," Nadina answered, "between a very pretty pair and these I have on which have low heels."

"That is what I would have expected you to choose," Lyle Westley said. "And now we have some way to walk, so let us get going."

He walked, as he spoke, up a twisting path which led them to the top of the cliffs.

There was no sign of a house.

But there were trees in blossom and it seemed a quiet, peaceful part of the country.

Lyle Westley walked on.

Nadina stopped only to pick some flowers that were growing wild.

He did not wait for her, but continued at an even pace.

She ran to catch up with him, saying:

"Look at these! They are so pretty and it is so exciting that we have got away."

"We are not safe yet," Lyle Westley said warningly. "We must pray that our luck will hold."

"I am sure it will," Nadina said. "I was thinking last night before I fell asleep that Papa must have guided you to the terrace so that I could save you and you could save me."

"Touch wood!" Lyle Westley exclaimed. "I think your Father must be very proud of you because you are behaving exactly as I hoped you would."

"What did you hope?" Nadina asked curiously.

"That you would do exactly as I told you to do," Lyle Westley replied, "and also to look on this as an adventure."

Nadina's eyes twinkled.

"I knew you were thinking I might behave like an hysterical woman and undoubtedly talk when we were moving down the Bosporus."

"I did remember," Lyle Westley confessed, "that I had not warned you that silence was important."

"Papa taught me that when I was about two," Nadina answered, "and Mama and I always obeyed him."

Walking on, Lyle Westley thought that if he had to rescue a woman as well as himself, he was exceedingly fortunate in having the daughter of Richard Talbort.

He had been afraid of having with him some woman who would cling to him if anything unexpected happened, and doubtless express over and over again how terrified she was.

Nadina was hurrying beside him with the flowers she had picked in her hand.

Her eyes behind the spectacles were taking in the beauty and the solitude of the countryside.

In fact, she was actually enjoying herself.

He could not imagine any of the women who had pursued him in London, or for that matter anywhere in the world, behaving so naturally.

They would have been shivering, and speaking of nothing but the danger they were in.

"She is certainly a unique member of her sex," he told himself.

He was determined, if it was humanly possible, to get her to England.

They walked on, and now in the distance they could see roofs.

"What shall we say if we are asked how we reached here?" Nadina enquired.

"That we were very fortunate," Lyle Westley replied, "in being given a lift by somebody who respected my cloth and who was coming in this direction in his wagon."

Nadina nodded.

"I do not suppose anybody will be interested," she said, "but I like to be aware of the whole story, just in case we get questioned."

"That is sensible," Lyle Westley approved.

He looked ahead to say:

"I made enquiries before left Constantinople, and there is an Inn of some sort where we can stay if the Ferry is not available until to-morrow."

Nadina glanced at him.

She thought, however, that any delay was unfortunate.

The further they could get from Constantinople the better.

By this time she knew that the maid-servant in Nannk Osman's house who usually called her would have found her bed had not been slept in.

She suspected the woman would go first to Rahmi's room to see if she was there.

Then, when the child began to ask for her, the maid might go downstairs.

She would ask the wives if they had seen her.

Last of all, because they were all frightened of him, they would tell Nannk Osman that she was missing.

Alternatively, he might discover it first.

If he chose to swim before breakfast, as he sometimes did, he would find her nightgown and the muslin robe.

Beside them would be the soft slippers and the towel.

He would not at first think she was drowned.

He would look out over the shining waters of the Bosporus to see her head as she swam in its cool waters.

Only as time passed and there was no sign of her would he become anxious.

'He was kind to me in his own way,' she thought.

With a little pang of her heart she thought of Rahmi.

She would never see the child again.

She hoped that nobody would be foolish enough to tell Rahmi that she had been drowned.

Then she remembered her Father saying, when they stayed in a place for any length of time and grew to love the people:

"It is no use looking back. We cannot alter the past, but there is always hope for the future."

Deliberately Nadina tried not to think of Rahmi.

Then she saw ahead of her a few unimpressive cottages.

Beyond them was a slightly larger building.

As they drew nearer still, she could see the glimmer of the water of the Dardanelles.

She wondered if the Ferry was in port.

She could see that Lyle Westley was also looking in that direction and guessed he was asking himself the same question.

They walked on in silence.

Now there were a few people moving towards what looked like a shop tucked away beyond the cottages.

It was easy to see where the passengers from the Ferry would land.

At the moment the harbour was empty.

There were only a few men seated by the water's edge, smoking and talking to each other.

Lyle Westley went straight to the Inn.

It was larger than it had seemed at first.

The ceilings were low and beamed, but the place was clean.

The Proprietor was a large, jovial-looking Turk.

"What can I do for you, Mister?" he asked Lyle Westley.

He was taking in, Nadina noticed, his cassock and speaking, she thought, with slightly more reverence in his voice than he would use to anyone else.

"Good-morning!" Lyle Westley said. "My sister and I are wishing to take the Ferry to Canakkale."

"Then you'll be disappointed!" the Innkeeper replied. "There be no Ferry 'til to-morrow, as one went yester even."

"That makes things difficult for us," Lyle answered, "but I hope you will be kind enough to oblige us with two rooms where we can stay the night."

"I've got two," the Innkeeper answered, "but I have a rule, which I hopes you'll understand, that the people who stay in my Hotel pay first."

"Of course," Lyle Westley replied, "and I think that is a very sensible precaution."

The Innkeeper appeared surprised at the answer.

However, he said how much he required and Lyle Westley put the money down promptly on the desk.

"As we have had a long journey to reach here," Lyle said conversationally, "I think my sister is somewhat fatigued and should rest."

Having put the money swiftly into his pocket, the Turk hurriedly and obsequiously took them up the uncarpeted stairs.

There was a passage going in both directions.

Turning left, he showed them into two rooms. They were small and bare but the beds looked clean.

Nadina realised she was, in fact, very tired.

The Landlord turned away to open the door of the room next to hers to show Lyle Westley where he would sleep.

Nadina sat down on the bed.

She may have slept last night, but was still tired.

She was sure, however, that Lyle Westley's solicitation for her was simply because he wanted to keep her out of sight.

The same reason doubtless applied to him.

She heard the heavy footsteps of the Proprietor going down the stairs.

Then Lyle Westley came into her room.

"You must rest," he said.

"And so must you," she answered. "I do not suppose you slept last night, even if I did."

"It is always wise to sleep when you have the opportunity," he replied. "Get into bed now while I go downstairs to see if I can find you some sort of breakfast."

He went towards the door, then stopped.

"Incidentally," he said, "it would be a mistake to call me 'Lyle.' "

Nadina's eyes widened.

"I forgot to ask you who we were," she said.

"Davis," he said. "I am Matthew Davis, and you are my sister Matilda."

Nadina laughed.

"Why 'Matilda'?"

"I have known two Missionaries of that name," Lyle replied.

"Very well," Nadina said, "I will be Matilda and try to behave as Matilda would."

"The trouble is," Lyle said, "that you do not look like a Matilda, so the longer you stay up here, the better."

He did not wait for an answer, but shut the door.

Nadina laughed.

It was what she had thought was the reason for him saying she must rest.

Actually she was only too willing to oblige.

She opened the suit-case to find that what she had seen down by the bay was correct.

There was one very dull brown dress and a night-gown of thick cotton.

It was so concealing that she thought it was exactly what a Missionary would think was proper.

'I am sure "Matilda" would be shocked at the diaphanous nightgowns I have left behind!' Nadina thought.

Laughing, she put on the nightgown and got into bed.

Some time later there was a knock on the door and Lyle came in.

He was carrying a tray on which there were two poached eggs besides some coarse bread, butter, and honey.

There was also a large cup of coffee, to which a little milk had been added.

Nadina looked at the tray and laughed.

"An English breakfast!" she exclaimed. "Or what Papa always told me the English eat."

"I cooked it myself," Lyle said. "I did not fancy anything I was offered, and because the Turk who is in charge of the kitchen wanted me to say a prayer for his sick Mother, he allowed me to do as I wished."

Nadina looked at him.

"And will you say a prayer for her?"

"Of course I will!" Lyle replied. "But I doubt if it will be answered."

"I think it will," Nadina said quietly. "Papa and Mama always prayed when we were in a tight corner with the Russians approaching. Their prayers were answered and we escaped."

She spoke with a sincerity that Lyle found rather touching.

She had not taken off her wig but, even wearing it, she had a radiance about her.

Her eyes seemed to have caught the sunlight.

"Eat your breakfast!" he said abruptly, and walked to the window.

He looked out.

With the exception of the men smoking by the sand, it appeared quiet and peaceful.

However, he knew how deceptive that could be, how easily the whole picture could change and, without any warning, they could be running for their lives.

They could end up hiding in some obscure place where they hoped they would never be found.

'Perhaps I should pray that the Battleship will reach us,' Lyle thought.

He knew without turning round that was what Nadina was doing.

*   *   *

Nadina awoke and saw to her surprise that it was seven o'clock in the evening.

She had slept all through the day.

Now she felt refreshed and also, not surprisingly, hungry.

She got out of bed and knocked on the wall, as Lyle had told her to do.

A minute later he opened the door.

"Well, Mrs. Rip Van Winkle," he said. "How do you feel?"

Nadina, who had got back into bed, smiled at him.

"I feel wonderful!" she said, "except that my tummy is empty."

She used an expression that Rahmi often used, and Lyle laughed.

"Get dressed," he said, "and do not forget to put on your spectacles, while I go downstairs and see what we can have for supper."

He came back ten minutes later to say:

"The cook has promised us what sounds like a good meal, and I have also ordered a bottle of wine which is quite drinkable, so hurry."

"I am ready," Nadina answered.

She picked up the spectacles as she spoke and put them on as she walked across the room.

She laughed at the way Lyle Westley was looking her up and down.

He was expecting to find fault.

Instead, he said:

"Although I had something to eat at midday, I am hungry too, so let us make the most of what is waiting."

They went downstairs to what was the Dining-Room at the back of the Hotel.

It looked out onto an unkempt garden which was compensated by a profusion of wild flowers and several trees in blossom.

To Nadina's surprise, there were several other people in the Dining-Room.

They were all men, two at one table and three at another.

Nadina thought that they were working-class Turks.

They were talking loudly, most of them drinking the fruit-juice which Nannk Osman sold in his shops.

There was, however, the one exception.

Nadina knew at once that he was not a Turk, but either Greek or Italian.

He was drinking wine.

As she saw him lift his glass to his lips, he was looking at her.

Quickly she looked away.

She talked to Lyle across the table.

Yet she was aware that the Greek, which she was almost certain he was, was watching her.

As Lyle had said, the meal, if not exciting, was edible.

Because Nadina was hungry, she enjoyed every mouthful.

They talked to each other in a Balkan language which was a mixture of Hungarian and Rumanian.

Fortunately, Nadina knew it because it was from one of the places in which she had stayed for some time.

She had been ten years old when her Father worked there.

She knew that Lyle thought it a mistake to let anybody think they were English.

She thought, too, that it was clever of him to choose the language of a country which was predominantly Christian.

In consequence they doubtless sent missionaries to convert the Infidels.

They finished their last course.

As they did so, the Greek, who appeared to be slightly drunk, rose and came to their table.

"Are you a Preacher?" he asked Lyle Westley.

He had been talking in Turkish to his friends.

Now he spoke in his own language and apparently expected Lyle to know it.

"I am," Lyle replied.

Without asking their permission, the Greek drew up a chair and sat down.

"I am Greek," he said unnecessarily, "and I wonder how you can waste your time on these savages, who have no idea how to behave."

Nadina was surprised.

She knew that the Turks hated the Greeks.

It seemed strange, however, that a Greek should come to Turkey and speak in such an offensive manner.

Lyle obviously thought the same thing, because he said quietly:

"I think you should be careful of what you say here!"

"This lot don't understand anything but their own rotten language," the Greek replied. "Where are you going?"

"To Canakkale, as soon as the Ferry will take us there," Lyle replied good-humouredly.

"The Ferry will be here to-morrow," the Greek replied, "so perhaps we could go together."

"My sister and I have work to do when we reach the other side of the Dardanelles," Lyle answered, "and now I think we must bid you good-night, as we are both very tired."

He rose to his feet as he spoke and Nadina did the same.

"There's no hurry," the Greek objected. "Stay and have a drink with me."

"We have finished," Lyle said, "but there is a little left of the wine we had with our dinner which we hope you will enjoy."

He passed the bottle across the table to the Greek as he spoke.

Then with a quick glance at Nadina he walked towards the door.

She was about to follow him, when the Greek reached out and clutched hold of her hand.

"When your brother's gone to bed," he said in a low voice, "you come downstairs to me. I want to talk to you."

With a little difficulty, Nadina managed to extract her hand from his.

"I am sorry," she said politely, "but I am very tired."

Quickly she hurried after Lyle.

He had reached the door and was looking back to see what had happened to her.

They did not say anything, but walked up the stairs together.

When they reached her room he asked in English:

"What did that drunken swine say to you?"

"He wanted me to meet him when you had gone to bed."

"He's the sort of person you find in every Inn sooner or later," Lyle said scathingly. "Drinks too much, talks too much, and runs after any woman who is available."

"Perhaps he will behave better to-morrow, when he is sober," Nadina said.

"If he does not, I will throw him into the sea!" Lyle replied.

Nadina held up her hands.

"No, no," she exclaimed, "I know it would be a mistake to draw attention to ourselves."

"You are right, of course," Lyle admitted. "This all comes of having a pretty woman with me. I have always thought it was a mistake."

"Now you are being unkind!" Nadina complained.

"I know you cannot help it," Lyle replied, "so good-night and sleep well. If you want me, knock on the wall."

"I shall do that," Nadina said, "but I think it is unlikely."

They smiled at each other and Lyle left her to go into his own room next to hers.

She locked her door, then undressed.

Lastly, before she got into bed, she removed the wig.

She felt it would be a relief to sleep without it.

Also, she had no wish to make it look rough and untidy in the daytime.

She placed it carefully over the bottle for drinking water on the wash-hand-stand.

It made an excellent support for a wig.

Then she got into bed and shut her eyes.

She was almost asleep when there was a sudden sound which startled her.

She wondered what it could be.

Then she was aware with a sense of horror that somebody was climbing in through her window.

She sat up in bed.

She had left the curtains undrawn because of the heat.

Now she saw, climbing into her room, there was a man.

The moonlight made it easy to recognise him as he came towards her.

She gave a cry of horror as she realised it was the Greek.

chapter six

LYLE did not get undressed except to take off his cassock.

The windows were wide open to let in what air there was.

Wearing only a shirt and trousers, he was studying a map of the coast by the light of a candle.

He was planning exactly where they would wait for the Battleship.

It was then he heard a scream and could hardly believe that it came from Nadina.

He jumped off the bed and turned towards the door.

As he did so, he remembered he had waited in the passage to hear her turn the key in the lock.

Then his brain was working quickly.

He recalled that while he had been sitting on his bed, he had heard a noise outside the window.

It was then that Nadina screamed again.

Lyle ran to the window and saw that outside there was the sloping roof of a verandah.

It took him only a few seconds to climb out of his own window and, holding on to the wall, to reach Nadina's.

As he sprang into the room he saw that the Greek was lying on top of Nadina.

She was struggling to be free of him, moving her head from side to side as she screamed.

In two strides Lyle was across the room.

Reaching the Greek, he pulled him off Nadina.

He then hit him on the chin with all his strength.

The man fell backwards onto the floor.

Lyle then pulled him to his feet and hit him again.

Holding him half-conscious with one arm, he unlocked the door and dragged him out of the room.

For one moment it passed through his mind that he might have thrown the man out of the window.

Then he knew that if he did so, he would be likely to break a leg.

It would cause a great commotion, and any number of questions would be asked.

He remembered how Nadina had said they must not draw attention to themselves.

He therefore hesitated.

The Greek started to slide from his arms onto the floor.

Lyle picked him up again and carried him to his own bed-room.

As he put him down on the floor, the Greek made a sound as if he was regaining consciousness.

Lyle hit him again.

He slumped back and was still. Lyle bound his legs together, then his hands behind his back.

He tied a gag behind his head.

Shutting the bed-room door behind him, Lyle went into Nadina's room.

She had got out of bed and was standing waiting for him.

When he appeared she rushed towards him and hid her face against his shoulder.

He put his arms round her.

"It is all right," he said quickly. "He will not trouble you again."

"H-he . . . frightened me! He was . . . horrible . . . bestial!"

The words were almost incoherent.

Lyle could feel her whole body trembling beneath the white nightgown he had chosen for her at the British Embassy.

His arms tightened.

He realised that this was the first time she had come into conflict with a man because she was a beautiful woman.

"It is all over now, and you have to be brave about this," he said soothingly.

As he spoke, he thought she had been extremely brave.

He knew what a shock it had been.

He had wanted to kill the Greek when he saw him lying on top of Nadina.

It was only his self-control that kept him from doing so.

He had been forced to kill a number of men in order to save himself when he was escaping from the Russians.

He felt justified in annihilating anyone who could hurt or spoil Nadina.

He suddenly realised that what he was feeling was strange, even to himself.

Then he knew, incredibly, that he had fallen in love.

Nadina's face was still buried in his shoulder.

He could feel the soft silkiness of her fair hair against his chin.

"It is impossible," he told himself, "for anyone to be so lovely and at the same time behave so well in such difficult circumstances."

She had obeyed every instruction he had given her before she left Osman's house.

She had not spoken on the long journey down the Bosporus and through the Sea of Marmara, nor had she made any complaint at what they had to do since.

"I love her!" he told himself. "But it is the last thing she must realise at this moment."

He knew it would only complicate further the situation they were in.

Very gently he moved Nadina back a step towards the bed.

She clung to him, saying:

"Suppose I had been . . . alone and . . . you had not . . . been here?"

"But I am here," Lyle said soothingly, "and now you have to help me think of what we must do about him before we leave."

He felt her stiffen, and she raised her head to look up at him.

"You . . . have not . . . killed . . . him?"

Lyle shook his head.

"No, but I wanted to do so."

"Wh-where is he?"

There was a nervous note in her voice which told him she was frightened the Greek might come to her again.

"At the moment," Lyle replied, "he is lying unconscious on the floor in my bed-room. There is unfortunately no cupboard in which I can lock him up for the night, but I have no wish for anyone to see the state he is in at this moment."

He felt Nadina tremble, but she was not crying.

He thought that any other woman in the same circumstances would be indulging in floods of tears.

"I tell you what I will do," he said quietly. "You get into bed and go to sleep. I will bring my mattress in here and stay with you. By the time the Greek regains consciousness we will have left the Hotel."

"The Ferry . . . will be . . . here?"

"It will arrive to-morrow morning at seven o'clock," Lyle said, "and we will be waiting for it."

"Y-you are quite sure h-he will not . . . come with us and . . . make a scene?"

"Quite sure," Lyle replied.

He felt her give a deep sigh of relief.

Then she said in a small voice:

"There is . . . no reason for . . . you to . . . come in here . . . with me. I will . . . shut the . . . window and I am . . . sure I will . . . be all right."

There was just a little hesitation in the last words which told Lyle how frightened she still was.

"I know what is best for you," he said, "and I want you to sleep and not lie awake, listening to strange noises. You must let me do things my way."

He thought again that few women would worry about his comfort when they were as frightened as Nadina was at this moment.

"Get into bed," he ordered.

He left the room, and going into his own saw that the Greek was in fact completely unconscious.

He was likely to remain so until morning.

Sprawled on the floor, he was an unpleasant-looking man of about thirty.

From the way he had behaved, Lyle was certain that he was used to being a success with women.

He had not expected any opposition from the sister of a Missionary.

He blew out the candle.

Picking up the mattress from his bed, he carried it and the pillow from his room into Nadina's.

Waiting for him, Nadina was thinking how terrifying it would have been if she had been travelling to England alone.

Her Father had never allowed any man he could not trust near her.

She had therefore never imagined someone who had spoken just a few words to her would desire her as a woman.

When the Greek had come towards her, he had said:

"Now, don't be frightened, my pretty one. I'll make you happy as I fancy you've never been happy before."

He reached the bed and Nadina had cried:

"Go away! How . . . dare you come . . . into my room! Go away . . . at once!"

The Greek made a sound that was half a laugh and half an expression of delight.

Then he threw himself on top of her.

Because it was so hot, she was covered only by a thin sheet.

His hands went to the neck of her nightgown to try and tear it open.

It was then she screamed and struggled frantically against the Greek.

The weight of him on top of her held her body immobile.

Because she was so innocent, she had no idea exactly what he intended.

She only thought that for him to kiss her lips or touch her with his hands would be horrifying, in fact, the most revolting thing that could ever happen to her.

As she tried to struggle against him, Lyle came in through the window.

"He saved me! He saved me!" she whispered.

As she did so, he came in through the door carrying the mattress.

He dropped it on the floor beside her bed, as the room was so small.

Then he went back to lock his own door after first securing the window.

If the Greek managed to shout for help, he would not be heard.

When Lyle went back into Nadina's room, he locked the door behind him.

It was then that she asked:

"Is he . . . still unconscious?"

"Out for the count!" Lyle said. "You must not doubt my pugilistic powers. I had a very experienced teacher."

"It was . . . wonderful of . . . you to come . . . at once when you heard my . . . screams. I remembered . . . even though I was so . . . frightened, that I had . . . locked the . . . door."

"Which I thought at the time was very sensible of you," Lyle said. "But I blame myself for not checking whether it would be easy for anyone to climb in through the window from the roof of the verandah."

"I did not . . . think of it either," Nadina confessed, "and Papa always looked around the rooms we occupied when we were travelling so that . . . the Russians could not . . . spring out . . . at us . . . unexpectedly."

"You are making me feel ashamed of myself," Lyle complained.

He put his pillow at the opposite end of the mattress.

When he lay down he could look at Nadina in the bed above him.

By the light of the moon coming through the window she was very beautiful.

Her fair hair was falling over her shoulders.

Lyle had not realised it was so long.

He could also see where the Greek had dragged at the neck of her nightgown, tearing the material.

Because she was so unselfconscious, he thought she was not aware of her beauty.

This was, however, further proof of how in many ways she was almost childlike.

He thought how different the idea of him sleeping in her room would have been with other women.

They would either, and this was more usual, be waiting impatiently for him to approach them, or they would be trying to look as desirable as possible.

If, on the other hand, Nadina had really been the sister of a Missionary, she would have been shocked at the impropriety of him, being a man.

She would doubtless have expected him therefore to be blind-folded.

He wanted to laugh at his thoughts.

But he was aware that his whole body was throbbing with the love he felt for Nadina.

The intensity of it took him by surprise.

Ever since he had known her he had been concerned first for his safety, then for hers.

The fact that they were human beings had not entered into his calculations.

But now he desired her and wanted more than anything in the world to kiss her and tell her how lovely she was.

Yet he would not have been who he was if he had not had an iron self-control over everything he did.

As he looked at Nadina he knew that anything he felt for her had to wait until he had taken her to safety.

Then and only then would he feel free to woo her as a man in love.

"Thank . . . you for . . . being so . . . kind to . . . me," Nadina said softly. "I do hope . . . you are . . . not too . . . uncomfortable."

"I promise you I am just as comfortable here as I should be next door," Lyle said. "So go to sleep, for I am going to wake you very early."

She knew he was as eager as she was to have left Eceabat before the Greek was discovered and before he was capable of complaining of the way he had been treated.

"I must just . . . say my prayers . . . again," Nadina answered. "I had . . . already thanked God for . . . bringing us here so safely, and also told . . . Papa how . . . grateful we are. Now I have to . . . thank Papa again for . . . sending you to . . . rescue me."

She smiled at him in the moonlight before she added:

"I am sure our . . . Guardian Angels are . . . watching over . . . us both."

Her voice was soft and sweet.

Despite what she had been through, she was smiling.

Lyle felt the blood throbbing in his temples.

"Good-night, Nadina," he said in a deep voice, "and dream of happy things."

"I will try to," Nadina answered, "and thank you, thank you . . . more than I can ever . . . say in words for . . . being here with . . . me."

She turned over as she spoke, and her face was towards the wall.

All Lyle could see was the back of her head and the long strands of her hair falling over her shoulders.

He deliberately turned on his side so that he could not look at her.

"I love her as I have never loved a woman before!" he told himself.

Then he forced himself to think of to-morrow and where they should go when they left the Ferry.

*   *   *

Nadina was fast asleep when she was awoken because Lyle was moving.

He had opened the door and was carrying the mattress back to his own room.

For a moment she wished she could sleep a little longer.

Then she remembered the Greek and sat up in bed.

She wondered if he had recovered consciousness.

If he had managed to free himself, perhaps he would attack Lyle when he opened the door of the room.

Or he might by some means of his own have moved out during the night.

Perhaps he was already making trouble, telling the proprietor and anyone else who would listen how he had been assaulted.

She wanted to go and see for herself if he was still there.

Then she remembered she was wearing only her night-gown.

Lyle would doubtless come back at any moment.

He appeared a second later, and she looked at him apprehensively.

"It is all right," he said, "the Greek is still unconscious and snoring most unpleasantly. The sooner we are dressed and downstairs, the better!"

He was speaking in a low voice.

Nadina knew it was because he did not wish to be overheard.

She therefore did not speak, but only nodded to show that she understood.

As soon as he left the room, she sprang out of bed.

Quickly she washed and slipped on the gown she had worn yesterday.

It was her own and she had no time to try on anything else.

Lastly she arranged the wig over her hair and put on her hat.

There was only the night-gown to pack away in the suit-case and the brush and comb.

Lyle had remembered to supply her with these from the British Embassy.

She was just shutting the suit-case when he came into the room.

"I have seen the Cook," he said, "and arranged for breakfast—of a sort, but it will not be so palatable as it was yesterday."

"If we had time," Nadina said, "I would like to have cooked breakfast for you. After all, it is a woman's job."

"It is something we shall do another time," Lyle promised, "but now we must hurry."

He picked up the suit-case and went from the room.

Nadina followed him.

As they passed his room she saw that the door of it was closed and the key was on the outside.

She knew he had locked the Greek in to make sure they were away from the Hotel before he regained consciousness.

There was nobody else in the Dining-Room.

As Lyle had said, the breakfast was a strange one.

It consisted of cold meat, pieces of cheese, and some black olives.

Nadina ate it all because she felt it was the sensible thing to do.

She also drank the coffee which was the same as she had the previous morning.

Lyle did the same.

Then, before she finished, he left the room to see if the Ferry had arrived.

He had only to look outside the front-door.

He came back to say it was just in sight and should be there within five minutes.

Nadina gave a sigh of relief.

Then she poured out another cup of coffee both for Lyle and herself.

Although he gave no sign of it, she knew he was waiting impatiently for them to leave.

She wondered if he was anxious only about the Greek, or perhaps for other reasons.

She knew, however, that it would be a mistake to ask questions.

After he had drunk his coffee, Lyle again went to the front-door.

When he came back he said:

"Now we can move."

Nadina jumped up from the table.

As they reached the Hall she saw the Proprietor waiting for them.

Lyle held out his hand.

"Thank you very much," he said, "for having my sister and me to stay with you. It has given us a much-needed rest, and we are very grateful."

"It has been nice to have you," the Proprietor replied, "and I hope I shall see you again."

Lyle picked up the suit-case he had put down as they shook hands, saying:

"That is certainly a possibility."

He walked outside, and Nadina, following him, said good-bye to the Proprietor.

Once outside, she could feel the sun was very warm.

Everybody in the village appeared to be there to see the Ferry arrive.

It was obvious that it was the one excitement in the lives of those who lived in Eceabat.

First the passengers on the Ferry disembarked, and there were only a few of them.

Then there were a number of crates to be unloaded, also several goats which, as they were frightened, gave those in charge of them a great deal of trouble.

At last it was obvious there were no more arrivals.

Lyle, still walking ahead, went up the gang-plank first, carrying the suit-cases.

He found a place for Nadina to sit which she realised was behind some superstructure.

She could therefore not be seen by those coming aboard.

She thought it was wise of Lyle to try and make them as invisible as possible.

At the same time, she was aware that, if there were Russians on the Ferry, it would be impossible for them to escape.

She tried to tell herself that she was being needlessly apprehensive.

Who was likely in Constantinople to guess where they were now?

And yet, instinctively, she was aware that although he did not show it, Lyle was tense.

Nearly half-an-hour later the Ferry started to move away on its journey across the Dardanelles.

Only then did Nadina know that Lyle had relaxed.

It was not a very long journey, for this was the narrowest part of the Strait—just one mile wide.

At the same time, there was no hurrying the Ferry.

It chugged along so slowly that Nadina hardly felt they were moving.

At last, however, they reached Canakkale.

She could see that it was very different from Eceabat.

By the Quay where they landed there were a few wagons and carts.

The wagons were needed for the goods which had been put on board before the Ferry left.

Lyle, however, quickly commissioned one of the open carts.

He looked at the stout young horse which was pulling the cart and said to the driver:

"Would you be prepared to take my sister and me a little further on from the Town?"

The young Turk, who was little more than a boy, grinned at him.

"Depends what you pay me!" he answered.

"We want to go to Intepe," Lyle replied.

The boy scratched his head.

"That's about nine miles," he remarked, "on the way to Troy."

"That is right," Lyle agreed, "and I am prepared to pay you what you ask for taking us there."

The boy gave him a sideways glance.

He then mentioned a sum which Nadina was certain was more than he expected.

Lyle deliberately hesitated.

"I am not a rich man," he said, "but as we want to get to Intepe I suppose I must accept your price."

The boy was obviously delighted.

He helped Lyle with the suit-cases.

When everything was in the cart, he drove off with a flourish.

After Eceabat, which had been a dull and sordid little village, Canakkale was beautiful.

Everywhere there were Judas trees in blossom.

They looked, Nadina thought, lovely.

Yet they bore a name from which everybody recoiled because it was the legendary tree on which Judas had hanged himself.

They went down a hill into the Town with purple blossom on either side of them.

The sea beyond was glittering in the sunshine.

It was difficult to think of anything unpleasant, or that they themselves might be in danger.

They drew nearer to the sea.

There were a number of ships of every shape and size.

Nadina guessed that some were coming back from Constantinople.

Others were moving Southwards through the Aegean into the Mediterranean.

There were also fishing-boats and quite a number of *Caiques* of every size.

She would like to have stayed in Canakkale for a little time to study what she knew was its great history.

Vaguely at the back of her mind she remembered what her Father had told her.

It was from near here Lord Byron had swum the course that the legendary Leander was supposed to have taken when he swam to Hero.

She longed to talk to Lyle about it.

But as he was silent, she imagined he had some reason for wishing to remain so.

She noticed he had brushed his hair even further over the sides of his forehead.

It gave him a completely different appearance from when it was brushed back.

She noticed, too, that he did not sit upright, looking about him, but lowered his chin so that passers-by could not see much of his face.

In fact, he might have been praying.

"I am sure he thinks we are in danger," Nadina told herself.

She pulled her hat a little lower down on her forehead, feeling suddenly once more afraid.

As she had done before, she slipped her hand into Lyle's and felt his fingers respond.

He also turned his head to look at her.

As he smiled, she thought the sun was brighter, and surprisingly she was no longer frightened.

They drove through the Town, then were out in the open country.

The road, which was not particularly well-kept, ran beside the sea.

Occasionally there was a little clump of cottages.

They looked as if they might belong to fishermen.

Otherwise, there were trees, a certain amount of undergrowth, and patches of bare land.

The heat of the sun was now much stronger.

Even the horse was tiring a little by the time they reached Intepe.

At the first sight of it, Nadina thought it could not be the place they were seeking.

It was, in fact, very much like the village they had left on the other side of the Dardanelles.

There were just a few scattered cottages.

She thought, however, that in the middle of them somewhere would be an Inn of some sort, or Hotel.

She wondered if it would be like the one in which they had stayed the previous night.

She only hoped there would not be a Greek visitor.

She tried to reassure herself that that was an experience that could happen only once on a journey.

It was unlikely to be repeated.

And anyway, Lyle was with her.

Without realising it, her fingers tightened in his and he said quietly:

"We have arrived and I am sure we shall be safe here."

He spoke in English so that their driver would not understand.

"Of course we will," Nadina replied.

She saw Lyle look away from her towards the sea.

Without him saying anything further, she knew that this was where the Battleship would pick them up.

As they drew nearer to Intepe she could see that the ground in front of the village sloped down towards the sea.

Further back, there had been, she was aware, high cliffs.

They drove into Intepe.

Without being told, the driver stopped at a quite large house compared to the others.

"I expect, being strangers," he said in his own dialect, "you'll be wanting somewhere to stay. This be the only place here where you'll get a bed."

"That is what we will want," Lyle agreed, "and thank you for bringing us here."

He got down from the cart and helped Nadina to the ground.

Then he lifted down the suit-cases.

He gave the driver the sum for which he had asked, and included a small tip.

The boy looked at it, then he said:

"Thanks, Sir! It's been a pleasure driving you and the pretty lady!"

Lyle did not answer.

He merely picked up the suit-cases and walked into the Inn.

As she followed him, Nadina thought he was annoyed.

Despite the fact that she was wearing a concealing wig and spectacles, the boy had still thought her pretty.

'Perhaps I should paint my nose red like a clown's,' she thought.

Then she wanted to laugh at the very idea of it.

Lyle found the Proprietor, a thin, rather dismal-looking man.

"I want two bed-rooms for about three nights," he asked.

Listening, Nadina thought they would not be staying as long as that.

Then she told herself that Lyle was taking no chances.

They might have nowhere to stay if the ship were delayed.

The Proprietor of the Inn did not answer immediately, as if he were thinking.

Then he said:

"I haven't got two rooms empty at the moment, but there's one double available."

There was hardly a pause before Lyle answered:

"We will take it, although my wife has a slight cold, which is why I had thought it best for us not to be together."

Suddenly Nadina felt a little shy.

It was something she had not been last night when Lyle had stayed with her because she was frightened by the Greek.

But to share a room deliberately, as if they were married, was something very different.

Then she told herself she was being foolish.

Lyle would be there to protect her, as he had last night.

Nothing mattered except that they got away.

She knew when they were driving in the cart that he was worrying.

The Russians, having discovered they were both missing from Constantinople, might somehow already be on their tracks.

"How can I be so foolish as to fuss about the proprieties?" she asked herself. "For, until the Battleship arrives to pick us up, we are in danger."

126

She was aware that Lyle was putting down a deposit on the room they had been offered.

The Proprietor seemed prepared to trust them for the rest.

A slovenly maid was then summoned from the kitchen to show them upstairs.

She did not offer to carry one of the suit-cases.

She flounced ahead, as if it were a nuisance to have more work at the Inn than she had already.

The room was larger than the one in which Nadina had slept last night, but not much.

There was a double bed which appeared comfortable.

The floor was bare of any carpets or rugs, and there were no curtains over the windows.

Yet it was clean and the windows looked out over the sea.

That, Nadina told herself, was what mattered more than anything else.

Lyle tipped the maid which seemed to surprise her.

She looked at the coin in her hand in astonishment before she said somewhat grudgingly:

"That's kind of you, Sir."

"We are grateful to have this comfortable room in which to rest," Lyle replied.

He accentuated the last word, and the maid said:

"No-one'll disturb you here. Nothing ever happens in Intepe—I can tell you that!"

Then, as if softened by his generosity, she asked.

"Is there anything I can get you?"

"What we would both like is something to eat," Lyle replied, "and I am sure you can cook fresh fish better than anybody else."

The woman laughed.

"Now you're flattering me, but I'll do my best and it'll be ready in half-an-hour."

"Thank you," Lyle said with a smile.

She hurried away.

As the door shut behind her they could hear her footsteps going down the stairs.

"If I get into trouble because I am too pretty, I am just seeing what a handsome man can do when he tries."

"You flatter me by saying it is my looks," Lyle replied, "but I fancy, if the truth is told, it is the first large tip she has had for a long time."

"If it comes under the heading of 'Bribery and Corruption,'" Nadina said, "it is worthwhile because I am very hungry."

"So am I," he answered, "and I am sure she will do her best, but if you would prefer me to go into the kitchen and help her, I will do so!"

Nadina laughed again.

"As your wife, you are deliberately trying to make me jealous!"

They both laughed, then Lyle said:

"Well, we have got here, and so far without any incident."

Nadina looked at him.

Then she said:

"You expected there would be one—why?"

There was silence, and she knew that Lyle was debating whether to tell her the truth or not.

Then he answered:

"I may be wrong, but I had a feeling that as we drove away from the Ferry after we had reached Canakkale there was a man watching the arrivals who did not look like a Turk."

Nadina gave a stifled scream.

"You mean . . . ?" she managed to ask, the words barely audible.

"I am almost certain," Lyle replied, "that he was a Russian!"

chapter seven

As they did not go downstairs, the maid, whose name was Gulizar, came to tell them that their meal was ready.

When she did so, Nadina looked at Lyle, and he said:

"As my wife is very tired, I will tell you what we will do. We will have a picnic here and I will help you to carry the trays upstairs."

"All right, Sir," Gulizar said, "but you'd better hurry or you'll spoil the fish I've taken such trouble over."

"I can see you are a very kind girl!" Lyle replied, which made her giggle.

They brought up the trays.

Nadina pulled out a small table into the centre of the room on which they could eat.

Although she was hungry, she was also apprehensive about what Lyle had said.

She thought, however, it would be a mistake to tell him she was frightened.

Instead, they ate quite a lot of the fish, which was excellent, before he said:

"I am afraid it will be rather boring for you, but I think it a mistake, unless it is absolutely necessary, for us to leave this room during the day."

"I expected you to say that," Nadina said in a low voice, "but I have no wish to go outside and keep . . . looking over . . . my shoulder."

"Then we will stay here," he said, "and anyway, it will be good for you to rest."

He wanted to stop her from feeling bored or frightened, so he began to talk.

He told her about Troy and other places he had visited.

Nadina found it enchanting.

She listened to everything he told her.

When they had finished their meal, Lyle packed the trays together and carried them downstairs.

He found Gulizar alone in the kitchen.

When he had gone there before, there was an old woman helping her.

He realised she did everything in the house, from the cooking to tidying the bed-rooms.

Casually he asked:

"Who else is staying here?"

"Nobody you'd fancy!" Gulizar replied. "Two German tourists who find fault with everything they're given to eat, and a man who writes History Books and is on his way to Troy."

Lyle thought she meant an Archaeologist. He at least sounded harmless.

However, he decided he would take no chances.

Having thanked Gulizar and flattered her, which left her in a fit of giggling, he went upstairs.

He told Nadina what he had discovered and added:

"I still think it would be wiser to stay here. I might go out later when it is getting dark and see if I can find the quickest way we can board the Battleship when it arrives."

"You are . . . quite certain . . . it will come . . . here?" Nadina asked nervously.

"The message I sent from Constantinople made it very clear that we would be at Intepe," he replied.

There was silence for a moment.

Then Nadina said:

"You do not think the . . . man you saw when we . . . landed from the Ferry . . . recognised . . . you?"

"It would not be a question of that," Lyle replied. "He would merely have been notified by those in the Third Section who are looking for me that I might be crossing the Dardanelles."

He paused before he said, almost beneath his breath:

"There is no reason why they should suspect that I was leaving for England on a Battleship."

"They will also not imagine that you have disguised yourself as a Missionary," Nadina said.

They talked during the afternoon, then once again Lyle went downstairs to collect their supper.

It was not as tasty as the midday meal had been.

Gulizar was having to feed the other guests staying at the Inn who had come back from their sight-seeing.

Lyle glanced at them as he passed the door.

He still thought it wise for Nadina to stay upstairs.

Even wearing the brown wig and spectacles she would still attract attention.

The guests might be asked questions without them realising it was of any importance.

When supper was over and the sun had sunk on the horizon, he said:

"Now I am going outside."

"Do you think that is . . . wise?" Nadina asked. "Suppose they are . . . waiting for you and you . . . never came . . . back?"

"I swear to you," he replied in a deep voice, "that I will be very careful of myself because I am looking after you."

Nadina wanted to beg him to stay.

Yet she knew he thought it important that, if they had to hurry to the beach, they should know the way.

She therefore forced herself to say nothing.

Lyle went to the window.

He waited until the sun had set in a blaze of glory.

Now it was dusk.

The first stars were appearing overhead.

But there was not enough light to see anything, just the way from the Hotel to the sea.

To Nadina's surprise, Lyle took off his cassock.

He was wearing underneath it a white shirt and long black trousers.

He went to the suit-case which he had not unpacked.

He drew out a black jacket and put it on.

Then he produced a black scarf which he wound round his neck.

He saw Nadina watching him with interest, and he explained:

"I shall move in the shadows—I am a shadow. I promise you no one will see me."

"Please, please . . . take care of . . . yourself," she pleaded. "You know I . . . cannot lose . . . you."

There was a little throb in her voice which made him long to kiss her.

But he turned away and, with a wave of his hand, left the room.

When he had gone Nadina started to pray.

'Please . . . God . . . take care of . . . him. Please do not let the . . . Russians find . . . him.'

She also prayed that her Father would guide them so that they would reach the Battleship in safety.

"You know better than . . . anybody . . . Papa," she said, "the difficulties . . . facing us. We have . . . survived so far and we must . . . both get to . . . England."

She prayed so fervently that when the door opened she almost screamed.

When she saw who it was she gave a little cry of happiness.

It was Lyle, and as he came in she said:

"You are . . . back! You are . . . safe! Did anything . . . happen?"

"Nothing," he answered, "except that I now know the way to the beach, which is just ahead of us, and I am sure it will be easy for a ship to anchor in what is comparatively smooth and deep water."

He removed the scarf from his neck and said:

"There was no-one about to notice me except for some gulls, and thank goodness, they cannot talk!"

He made her laugh as he meant her to do.

Then he said:

"I thought you might have had the sense to undress while I was gone and get into bed."

Nadina blushed.

"I am sorry . . . it was . . . stupid of me . . . but I did not . . . think of it."

Because she thought he was criticising her, she added:

"I was . . . praying."

"That is what I thought you were doing," Lyle replied. "Undress now and let us sleep while we can. I will go downstairs and talk with Gulizar for exactly ten minutes!"

Nadina laughed, but she got off the bed.

As soon as she was alone, she undressed very quickly.

She could not help wondering where he would sleep.

It would be very unconventional, and would have shocked her Mother if she shared the bed with him.

She put on the white nightgown she had worn last night.

She had just got back into bed when Lyle returned.

He was carrying something over his arm, and as she looked at it curiously, he explained:

"I saw a door in the corridor was open, and this blanket was lying on the bottom of the bed, obviously not wanted by the person occupying the room."

"So you took it?" Nadina questioned.

"I took it to make myself comfortable," Lyle replied, "and I am sure you can spare me one of your pillows."

"Are you . . . going to . . . sleep on the . . . floor?" Nadina asked.

"That is what I intend to do," Lyle replied.

"But you did that last night, and it is only fair that you should have the bed to-night. I will sleep on the floor."

Lyle laughed.

"Do you really think I would agree to that? I assure you, I have slept in much worse places, including a cave which smelt of the wolves that had been in it before me."

Nadina gave an exclamation of horror, and he said:

"Now turn your face away and shut your eyes while I wash. I will then make my bed as comfortable as possible. I am sure, as you have two blankets and, as it is very hot, you can spare me one."

"I can spare them both," Nadina offered.

"One will be plenty," Lyle replied. "Now, shut your eyes like a good girl."

She did as he told her.

She could hear him pouring cold water into the basin.

He obviously washed himself thoroughly and, after what seemed a long time, he said:

"You can turn round now, although it is not a very edifying spectacle."

She opened her eyes.

When she turned round she saw that he was bare from the waist up.

He was wearing his long black trousers which were fastened round his waist with a belt.

Tucked into it was a revolver.

"D-do you . . . always carry . . . that?" she asked hesitatingly.

"I should be very stupid not to do so," Lyle replied, "especially when I have a beautiful Princess to protect from a large Dragon!"

She knew he was making light of the matter, and she answered:

"The Princess is very, very grateful to the . . . Knight who is . . . rescuing her."

Lyle took a pillow from the bed and put it down on the two blankets on the floor.

Then he said:

"Good-night, Nadina. Blow out the candle and dream of the excitement of seeing England for the first time."

"Good-night . . . Lyle," Nadina replied. "God bless . . . you."

She shut her eyes.

As she was thinking of how exciting it would be to travel with Lyle in a Battleship, she fell asleep.

*   *   *

Nadina awoke with a start, thinking it must be morning.

Then she realised it was still very dark.

She could hear Lyle breathing evenly on the floor beside her.

She thought how fortunate she was that he was there.

She was not afraid as she would have been if she were alone.

Then suddenly, almost like a stab in her heart, she was aware of danger!

It was such a strong feeling that she felt herself tremble.

She knew she had the same perceptive power her Father had.

Looking back, she could remember a dozen occasions when he had said suddenly and unexpectedly:

"We are moving immediately!"

"Moving?" her Mother exclaimed at first. "But why, darling? We are very comfortable here."

"We are in danger," her Father answered. "Pack your things as quickly as you can while I find something to convey us away before it is dawn."

Invariably he had been proven right.

They had learnt later the Russians had arrived to find them gone.

After that, Nadina and her Mother did exactly as he told them.

There were times when they were forced to leave behind things they cherished.

Her Father was saying:

"Hurry! Hurry! There is no time to lose."

Now Nadina felt as if he were guiding her.

She could almost hear his voice saying:

"Hurry! Hurry! Leave here immediately!"

Because it was so vivid, she said after a moment:

"Lyle! Lyle! Wake up!"

He was instantly alert because he was used to danger.

"What is it?" he asked.

"You may think I am being ridiculous," she answered, "but I know, as Papa used to know, that we are in danger and we must leave at once!"

She drew in her breath before she said:

"I can feel it coming . . . nearer and nearer to . . . us!"

Lyle got to his feet.

"Very well," he said, "dress quickly, and we will go down to a landing-place which I saw on the beach."

As he spoke, he was putting on his shirt.

Nadina got out of bed.

She had left her clothes tidily on a chair on the other side of the room.

She groped her way to it and started putting them on.

She could hear Lyle moving about, but she did not turn round.

When she had fastened her dress she asked:

"Shall I put on my wig?"

"It is unnecessary, as nobody will see us," Lyle replied. "We will stay on the beach until dawn. Then, if you think the danger is past, we can come back here."

Nadina thought that nobody else except for her Father would have been so understanding.

"You are ready?" Lyle asked.

"Yes," she replied.

They were speaking in very low voices so as not to disturb anyone sleeping in the next room.

Lyle went to the door and opened it silently.

The Inn was very quiet and, as Nadina joined him, she slipped her hand into his.

They went down the stairs on tip-toe.

They saw no one and, because it was dark, they had to feel their way.

Lyle drew Nadina to what she realised was the way to the kitchen.

When they reached it she could feel the heat from the stove and see the embers of a fire.

Lyle found the way to the back door.

Then they were outside.

It was dark, but now the stars gave just enough light to see their way.

To her surprise, however, Lyle did not go directly towards the beach as she had expected.

Instead, he walked some distance away from the sea, then made a detour through a clump of trees.

At last he turned towards the sea.

Now Nadina understood what he was doing.

He was approaching the beach from a different direction.

If by any chance they were seen, no one would realise they had come from the Hotel.

Lyle was wearing his black coat, not his cassock.

She was sure if there were any spies about, they would not connect them with the man and woman they had seen coming from the Ferry.

However, Nadina thought unhappily, one could never be sure of anything.

Now Lyle was helping her down onto the beach about which he had spoken earlier.

It was quite large with some rough boats pulled from the sand onto the pebbles.

Then the land rose on each side until it was level with the houses beyond it.

Lyle helped her over the pebbles.

At what seemed a corner of the beach there was a large clump of shrubs.

They were in blossom and had a pungent scent.

As they reached them, Nadina knew that this was the hiding-place Lyle had found.

He parted the shrubs and, without being told, Nadina crawled through them.

In the centre there was a sandy place where she could sit down.

As soon as she had done so, Lyle joined her.

He had released the shrubs and they closed over their heads.

They were encompassed with a screen of green leaves and white blossoms.

He put his arm around her so that she could lean against him.

Now for the first time she spoke since they had left the Hotel.

"This was . . . clever of . . . you!"

"I thought in some strange way," he answered, "when I first saw them that they might be useful."

"Perhaps I am . . . wrong and there is . . . nothing to . . . frighten us," Nadina said.

"We were right to take no chances," Lyle answered. "I, too, have been aware of danger, but I had no wish to leave the Hotel until the Battleship arrives."

"Suppose it is . . . delayed?" Nadina asked in a frightened tone. "We cannot . . . stay here in the . . . daytime."

"In this sort of situation," Lyle said in a quiet voice, "one has to take one step at a time. You were very wise and brave in telling me we were in danger, and I believe you. Therefore we must just pray, as I know you have been praying, that the Battleship will be here soon."

"You . . . understand," Nadina said. "I know it could only be a man . . . like Papa who could . . . understand the sort of . . . feelings that . . . most people . . . would . . . laugh . . . at."

"We will laugh when we reach England," Lyle said quietly.

She put her head on his shoulder.

She thought how lucky she was to have anyone so kind to look after her.

Most men would have been annoyed at being woken up by a woman.

They would have thought she was hysterical to suggest they must go out in the middle of the night and sit on the beach.

'I am lucky . . . so very . . . lucky to have . . . found him,' she thought.

Then she remembered the Greek and shivered.

Lyle's arms tightened.

"It is all right," he said. "I know, if you are being perceptive about danger, I am perceptive enough to know that we are going to win!"

He nearly added:

' . . . because I love you!'

Then he told himself that she was relying on him as a child relies on its Father.

What he must do was to make her feel safe and not trouble her with any other emotion.

At the same time, it was a bitter-sweet feeling to hold her gently when he wanted to crush her in his arms, to kiss her with passionate, demanding kisses until she kissed him in return!

'All that matters,' he thought, 'is that I get her to

safety, even if I die in doing so.'

Nadina snuggled closer to him and shut her eyes.

She was praying again that the Battleship would come for them soon.

At the same time, she was a little sleepy.

She was, in fact, almost, if not quite, oblivious as to where she was and what was happening.

Suddenly she felt Lyle's whole body stiffen.

She opened her eyes.

As she did so, she realised that dawn was just breaking and the sky was lightening.

She looked up at Lyle.

He had parted the shrubs in front of him and was glancing through the leaves towards the sea.

She looked in the same direction.

Although she could hardly believe it, she saw the outline of a Battleship against the sky.

"It has come!" she whispered.

"Do not move!" Lyle warned. "Keep silent!"

It was an order, and she looked at him in surprise.

She wanted to run down to the edge of the water and wave to those on the ship to attract their attention.

Lyle, however, was completely immobile, so she could only look and wait.

It seemed to her that an hour passed while they did so.

In reality, it was no more than fifteen minutes.

The light became stronger and the last stars began to fade.

Then she saw, coming from behind the ship, a boat.

It was being rowed by eight seamen, and she

could see quite clearly they were heading for the shore.

She thought Lyle must also have seen it.

Because he had not moved or spoken, she looked at him questioningly.

Then he said very quietly:

"When I tell you to do so, be ready to run. Do not look back. Just run as fast as you can and get into the boat."

The way in which he spoke surprised her, but she knew she must obey him.

Instinctively her hands went to her long skirt.

She pulled it up almost to her knees so that it would not be an encumbrance.

The boat had almost reached the shore, and at last Lyle said:

"Run!"

It was an order.

He parted the bushes as he spoke.

Nadina forced herself through them, first onto the pebbles, then onto the sand.

It was then she really started to run, not looking back but fixing her eyes on the boat.

Lyle gave her a good start before he followed her.

Even as he did so he saw the man whom he had sensed would be watching for the arrival of the Battleship.

He was silhouetted against the sky.

The man had been looking at Nadina.

But, as he saw Lyle, his hand went to the inside pocket of his coat.

Even as it did so, Lyle shot him through the head.

He fell backwards onto the sand.

As Lyle reached the boat, Nadina was being helped aboard.

He followed her, reaching out as he did so to force her down on the bottom of the boat.

"Move as quickly as you can!" he ordered the seamen.

As he spoke, those who had been holding it steady hauled themselves aboard.

They dipped their oars and started pulling out to sea.

Lyle, looking back, saw a second Russian who, as he had expected, had heard the report of the revolver.

He was running to the higher ground above the beach.

He had a pistol in his hand.

When he saw Lyle in the stern of the boat, he stopped and raised it to fire.

With his customary quickness, Lyle shot him through the heart.

As the Russian fell, his finger tightened on the trigger.

The bullet went harmlessly up into the air to fall into the sea.

The sailors were pulling the boat at a speed which brought it to the stern of the Battleship within a few minutes.

There was a rope-ladder over the Ship's side.

As Nadina started to climb it, Lyle was behind her, guiding her feet in case she fell.

Only as helping hands lifted her onto the deck did the full horror of what had just occurred overcome her.

She staggered against Lyle.

He picked her up in his arms as a Petty Officer said:

"This way, Sir!"

Lyle followed him.

They went below, and the Petty officer opened a cabin door.

"I'll tell th' Captain what has happened," he said.

Lyle carried Nadina into what he knew was the Captain's Night-Cabin with its usual big bunk-bed.

The cabin was larger than any other in the ship.

He set Nadina down on the bed.

When he would have moved away she put her arms around his neck.

"I-I thought . . . he would . . . kill you!" she said in a broken voice.

"Would you have minded?" Lyle asked.

She looked up at him and he saw there were tears in her eyes.

His lips came down on hers.

He kissed her as he had wanted to do for so long, passionately, demandingly, holding her tightly against him.

He had waited for this.

It was, he knew, even more wonderful than he had imagined it would be.

He felt his love for her sweep over him like a tidal wave.

At that moment the door of the cabin opened and the Captain came in.

Lyle took his arms from Nadina.

The Captain walked towards then saying:

"Good-morning, Sir Lyle! I was expecting you, but not quite so dramatically!"

Lyle held out his hand.

"I am very grateful to you for being there at just the right moment, Captain! And now will you please put to sea immediately?"

"We are already under way," the Captain replied, "and I am extremely thankful you were saved at what seems to have been the very last minute!"

The Captain then glanced towards Nadina and added:

"I was not aware that you had a lady with you."

"She is also escaping from Turkey," Lyle informed him. "I should be grateful, Captain, if, as soon as we are out to sea, you would marry us."

For a moment the Captain looked as if his breath had been taken away.

Then he said:

"Of course, Sir Lyle! It will be a great pleasure and, incidentally, it will solve the problem of how I can manage to provide you with another cabin!"

Lyle laughed.

"We are very grateful for yours, Captain!"

"May I suggest," the Captain said, "that your marriage should take place in about thirty minutes?"

"That will suit us admirably," Lyle replied.

The Captain went from the cabin with just one curious look at Nadina.

As he shut the door behind him, Lyle moved back towards her.

She looked up at him.

He thought, in the dawn light coming through the scuttle, that she looked too beautiful to be real.

"D-did you . . . say," she asked in a whisper, "that we are . . . to be . . . married?"

"I cannot wait any longer," Lyle replied, "to tell you how much I love you!"

"You . . . love me?"

There was an amazement in her voice which made him smile.

He sat down on the bed.

"I do not think I have ever suffered such agony as I have these past few days. They have seemed like a million years. I have been longing to kiss you and tell you how beautiful you are."

"I never guessed . . . never imagined . . . that you . . . loved me."

"What I am waiting to know," Lyle said, "is whether you love me."

"I do! Of course . . . I love . . . you," Nadina answered, "but I did not . . . know it was . . . love until you . . . kissed me."

She looked at him a little shyly and asked:

"H-how did you . . . know when you . . . have never . . . asked me . . . if I would . . . marry you?"

"I knew you loved me, even though you might not be aware of it," Lyle said. "You were always concerned for my safety, worrying about my comfort, and were so unbelievably brave."

"And you . . . knew it . . . was . . . love?" Nadina asked.

"I knew no-one could react like that in such a situation unless they loved me," Lyle replied, "and when I kissed you just now, I felt the love on your lips. We will, my darling, be very happy together."

"Suppose . . . you are disappointed?" Nadina asked.

"Do you really think I could be disappointed in you?" Lyle asked. "You are the most beautiful person I have ever seen in my life, beside being sweet, gentle, trusting, and braver than any other woman in the world!"

Nadina gave a little cry.

"Oh, please go on . . . thinking of me like . . . that?" she begged. "I love you because . . . you are so . . . brave and so . . . strong and I know that . . . without you . . . I would have wanted to . . . die!"

"You are not going to die," Lyle said. "You are going to live. We have a lot of work ahead of us, but I know it will be wonderful and like being in Heaven because we will be together."

"How can you . . . say such . . . things to . . . me?" Nadina asked.

Then it was impossible to speak because Lyle was kissing her, kissing her until the cabin seemed to swirl round them.

Their feet were no longer on earth but in the sky.

It was Nadina who came back to reality first.

"I must . . . tidy myself if we are . . . going to be . . . married," she said, "and please, Lyle, what are . . . we to do . . . about clothes?"

"I will buy you everything you need at the first Port of Call," he said, "and when we reach England you shall have the most beautiful trousseau any bride ever possessed."

"That will be . . . wonderful," Nadina exclaimed. "In the meantime, I have not even a . . . night-gown."

She looked up at him and saw Lyle's eyes twinkling.

Impulsively she hid her face against him.

"I shall be . . . very shy," she whispered.

"I adore you when you are shy," he answered.

Then, because she knew she must be practical, she got off the bed.

Going to where there was a looking-glass on the wall, she exclaimed with horror because her hair was untidy.

"You look beautiful!" Lyle said before she could speak. "And I am sure the Captain can provide you with a comb."

He found one for her which was by the mirror.

He realised that the Captain had emptied a number of drawers in the cabin for the clothes they had not brought with them.

"We will have to manage," he said, "until we reach Athens, or wherever else the Captain is going to call. The only thing that matters, my darling, is that at last I can make you mine."

Nadina blushed.

He was just about to take her into his arms when there was a knock on the door.

The Captain came in wearing, Lyle was aware, his Full-Dress Coat and his medals.

He was also wearing his cap with its gold braid and was carrying a Prayer-Book.

Lyle took Nadina by the hand and drew her to the other side of the cabin.

There was a table as well as two comfortable arm-chairs.

The ship was moving.

At the same time, the sea was smooth and they were not rolling.

"If you are ready, Sir Lyle," the Captain said, "I will join you and this lady in Holy Matrimony which, as Captain of this ship I am empowered to do. But I must first know the bride's name."

"It is Nadina," Lyle replied, "and my name is Lyle Alexander."

Nadina noticed that he did not give her a surname.

She thought perhaps he had a reason for not doing so.

For the moment, however, all she was concerned with was that she would be Lyle's wife.

She need never be afraid of being alone again.

The Captain read the Marriage Service in a quiet, serious voice.

Lyle took his signet ring from his little finger and put it on Nadina's.

Finally the Captain said:

"With the powers invested in me by Her Majesty Queen Victoria, as Captain of this ship, I now pronounce you man and wife."

Lyle put his arms around Nadina and kissed her gently.

Then he held out his hand.

"Thank you, Captain," he said, "and now you must meet my wife properly. She is as grateful to you as I am."

"I am very grateful!" Nadina said softly.

She thought the Captain was looking at her with admiration in his eyes.

Then he said:

"It is still early in the morning, and I doubt if you have had much sleep. I therefore suggest that we celebrate this very happy occasion with a bottle of champagne later in the day."

"An excellent idea!" Lyle replied.

"Is there anything you would like at the moment, Sir Lyle?"

"Later," Lyle replied, "I would like to talk to you about a great number of things we require, having come aboard with nothing but what we stand up in."

"I am sure, Sir Lyle, we can provide you with anything you need," the Captain replied. "It is going to be rather more difficult where your wife is concerned. But if we go at maximum speed we can anchor in the Piraeus, near Athens, to-morrow afternoon."

"I am sure we can manage until then." Lyle smiled.

The Captain bowed.

With a last look at Nadina, as if he could not believe she was so beautiful, he went from the cabin.

As soon as he had gone, Lyle put his arms round Nadina and drew her close to him.

"I love you, my darling," he said, "and I cannot wait any longer to tell you how much."

"Y-you are making me . . . shy," Nadina whispered, "so please . . . look away while . . . I undress."

"I will do that," Lyle said, "but I assure you I am never going to sleep on the floor again!"

She laughed.

He walked to the other side of the cabin, taking off his coat, flinging it down on one of the armchairs.

Nadina drew one of the curtains across the bunk-bed so that he could not see her.

Then, having taken off her clothes, she slipped into bed.

As she did so, she instinctively shut her eyes to say a prayer of gratitude because they were safe.

She was sure if she had not been warned of the danger, she and Lyle might easily have died in the Hotel.

Then she felt him beside her, taking her into his arms.

She would have hidden her face because she was shy at having no night-gown to wear.

Now Lyle was kissing her wildly, passionately, and more demandingly than he had done before.

She could feel the fire on his lips.

Because his hand was touching her and his kisses were so exciting, she felt a little flicker of flame moving within her.

She was conscious of sensations she had never imagined.

She knew it was part of the love and the ecstasy which her Father and Mother had felt for each other.

Love had made them run away together.

It was something they had never regretted through the twenty-one years they had been pursued by the Russian spies.

"I love you! I love you," she wanted to say to Lyle, "and no matter what happens in the future I will love you because we will be together."

She knew he was feeling the same.

Then, as he made her his, she thought that they had reached Heaven.

The rapture and wonder of it was inexpressible.

* * *

A long time passed.

The sunshine was pouring through the portholes

and the throb of the engines was like music beneath them.

It was then Lyle murmured:

"I have something to say to you, darling, but I do not want you to be hurt."

"Hurt? Why should I . . . be hurt?" Nadina asked.

He did not answer, and she looked up at him anxiously.

"Y-you are not . . . disappointed in me?"

He laughed, and it was a very tender sound.

"My precious, how can you imagine any such thing! You are perfect—the wife I have always dreamed was somewhere in the world. At last I have found you."

"Then . . . nothing else can . . . hurt me," Nadina said, "unless you . . . want to go . . . adventuring again. I do not think I . . . could bear . . . it!"

"That part of my life is finished," Lyle answered. "I have a great deal to do in England, and you will inspire and help me, so I need you desperately!"

"Then . . . what could . . . hurt me?" Nadina enquired.

"Because I do not want to have to worry about your safety," Lyle said, "although your Father is a hero in England, I do not wish anybody to know that you are his daughter."

Nadina looked at him in surprise. Then she said:

"I understand. At the same time, I am very . . . proud of Papa."

"He was one of the heroes of his age," Lyle said. "However, people talk, and what they say is reported in the newspapers!"

Nadina gave a little cry.

"I had not thought of that!"

"But I had," he said. "As you are aware, there is a Russian Embassy in London. Sooner or later, who you are will get back to St. Petersburg and the Third Section."

Nadina put out her hand to hold on to him.

"Then you would ... have to ... hide me all ... over again! Oh, Lyle, I understand, and of course ... no-one must ... know who I am."

"Not for the moment, at any rate," Lyle said. "Perhaps in the years to come we will be able to tell our grandchildren, and they will think it is the most exciting story they have ever heard."

Nadina gave a little smothered laugh that was almost a sob.

"We must have ... children ... first," she whispered, "and they must ... never be in danger ... as we have ... been."

"That is exactly what I was thinking, and so, my precious, we will think of a name which will satisfy everybody that you are of importance, but which will mean nothing to the Russians."

"You are right ... of course you are ... right," Nadina said, "and nothing matters ... except that I do not have to ... look over my shoulder ... every time I go out through a door ... or worry about ... you."

"I think once I am in England the Russians will give up their pursuit of me because it will prove too difficult. But you know as well as I do that they will never forgive your Mother for running away and not making a Royal marriage. She flaunted the Tsar, even though he was an abominable tyrant."

"Then I must ... no longer ... have any ...

Russian blood in me," Nadina said. "I will . . . just be a quiet . . . rather dull Englishwoman."

Lyle laughed.

"I knew when I kissed you and when I made love to you that you could never deny your Russian blood," he said. "My precious, that part of you excites me to madness. At the same time, we have to be sensible."

"Of course, darling," Nadina said. "And what is sensible is that I am your wife. I love you and, please God . . . we shall die of . . . old age and not from . . . anything else."

"Amen to that!" Lyle said. "Now, my adorable, precious little Russian Princess, I am going to give you a thousand kisses in Russian and it will be our secret, hidden from the world—hidden by our love from everybody but ourselves."

He felt Nadina's arms go round his neck, the softness of her body against his.

Then the fires were leaping within them both.

"God! How I love you." Lyle exclaimed, "I want you. Give me yourself."

"I am yours, darling!" Nadina murmured. "Love me . . . oh, Lyle . . . love me."

Once again they were flying towards a Heaven of their own.

It was hidden by the Grace of God from all those who would despoil it.

ABOUT THE AUTHOR

Barbara Cartland, the world's most famous romantic novelist, who is also an historian, playwright, lecturer, political speaker and television personality, has now written over 563 books and sold over six hundred and twenty million copies all over the world.

She has also had many historical works published and has written four autobiographies as well as the biographies of her mother and that of her brother, Ronald Cartland, who was the first Member of Parliament to be killed in the last war. This book has a preface by Sir Winston Churchill and has just been republished with an introduction by Sir Arthur Bryant.

Love at the Helm, a novel written with the help and inspiration of the late Earl Mountbatten of Burma, Great Uncle of His Royal Highness The Prince of Wales, is being sold for the Mountbatten Memorial Trust.

She has broken the world record for the last sixteen years by writing an average of twenty-three books a year. In the *Guinness Book of World Records* she is listed as the world's top-selling author.

Miss Cartland in 1978 sang an Album of Love Songs with the Royal Philharmonic Orchestra.

In private life Barbara Cartland, who is a Dame of the Order of St. John of Jerusalem, Chairman of the St. John Council in Hertfordshire and Deputy President of the St. John Ambulance Brigade, has fought for better conditions and salaries for Midwives and Nurses.

She championed the cause for the Elderly in 1956 invoking a Government Enquiry into the "Housing Condition of Old People."

In 1962 she had the Law of England changed so that Local Authorities had to provide camps for their own Gypsies. This has meant that since then thousands and thousands of Gypsy children have been able to go to School, which they had never been able to do in the past, as their caravans were moved every twenty-four hours by the Police.

There are now fourteen camps in Hertfordshire and Barbara Cartland has her own Romany Gypsy Camp, called Barbaraville by the Gypsies.

Her designs "Decorating with Love" are being sold all over the U.S.A. and the National Home Fashions League made her, in 1981, "Woman of Achievement."

She is unique in that she was one and two in the Dalton list of Best Sellers, and one week had four books in the top twenty.

Barbara Cartland's book *Getting Older, Growing Younger* has been published in Great Britain and the

U.S.A. and her fifth cookery book, *The Romance of Food,* is now being used by the House of Commons.

In 1984 she received at Kennedy Airport America's Bishop Wright Air Industry Award for her contribution to the development of aviation. In 1931 she and two R.A.F. Officers thought of, and carried, the first aeroplane-towed glider airmail.

During the War she was Chief Lady Welfare Officer in Bedfordshire, looking after 20,000 Servicemen and women. She thought of having a pool of Wedding Dresses at the War Office so a Service Bride could hire a gown for the day.

She bought 1,000 gowns without coupons for the A.T.S., the W.A.A.F.'s and the W.R.E.N.S. In 1945 Barbara Cartland received the Certificate of Merit from Eastern Command.

In 1964 Barbara Cartland founded the National Association for Health of which she is the President, as a front for all the Health Stores and for any product made as alternative medicine.

This is now a £65 million turnover a year, with one-third going in export.

In January 1988 she received *La Médaille de Vermeil de la Ville de Paris.* This is the highest award to be given in France by the City of Paris. She has sold 25 million books in France.

In March 1988 Barbara Cartland was asked by the Indian Government to open their Health Resort outside Delhi. This is almost the largest Health Resort in the world.

Barbara Cartland was received with great enthusiasm by her fans, who feted her at a reception in the City, and she received the gift of an embossed plate from the Government.

Barbara Cartland was made a Dame of the Order of the British Empire in the 1991 New Year's Honours List by Her Majesty, The Queen, for her contribution to Literature and also for her years of work for the community.

Called after her own beloved Camfield Place, each Camfield Novel of Love by Barbara Cartland is a thrilling, never-before published love story by the greatest romance writer of all time.

Barbara Cartland